THE
GHETTO
WITHIN

THE
GHETTO
WITHIN

A NOVEL

SANTIAGO H. AMIGORENA

Translated from the French by Frank Wynne

HARPERVIA

An Imprint of HarperCollins*Publishers*

Excerpt(s) from *If This Is a Man* by Primo Levi, translated by Stuart Woolf, copyright © 1958 by Giulio Einaudi editore S.p.A.; translation copyright © 1959 by The Orion Press, Inc. Used by permission of Viking Books, an imprint of Penguin Publishing Group, a division of Penguin Random House LLC. All rights reserved.

English translation copyright © 2022 by Frank Wynne.

HarperCollins books may be purchased for educational, business, or sales promotional use. For information, please email the Special Markets Department at SPsales@harpercollins.com.

Originally published as *Le Ghetto intérieur* in France in 2019 by Éditions P.O.L.

FIRST HARPERVIA EDITION PUBLISHED IN 2022

Designed by SBI Book Arts, LLC

Library of Congress Cataloging-in-Publication Data has been applied for.

ISBN 978-0-06-301833-4
ISBN 978-0-06-327720-5 (ANZ)

22 23 24 25 26   LSC   10 9 8 7 6 5 4 3 2 1

For Mopi, who wrote it before I did

For Marion, who is writing it with me

To react commensurately to the incommensurable was impossible. Those who demanded this of the victims might just as well demand of a fish floundering on a bank that it promptly grow legs and walk back to its watery kingdom.

—Günther Anders, *We Sons of Eichmann*

PREFACE

Twenty-five years ago, I began writing a book to oppose the silence that has stifled me since birth. Of this book, which comprises six parts, the following have been published: part one, *A Laconic Childhood*; the second chapter of part two, *A Voiceless Youth*; part three, *A Taciturn Adolescence,* published as two separate volumes, *The Second Exile* and *First Times*; part four, *A Mute Maturity,* also published as two separate volumes, *First Love* and *First Defeat*; and three appendixes (1978; 2003, published as *Days I Have Not Forgotten*; and 2086, published as *My Last Words*). The pages you now hold in your hands are the source of this literary project.

IN BUENOS AIRES, THE AFTERNOON OF SEPTEMBER 13, 1940, was rainy and the war in Europe so remote that one might still have thought it was peacetime. Avenida de Mayo, the broad thoroughfare lined with art deco buildings that connected the presidential palace to the National Congress, was all but deserted; only a few men, scurrying from their city center offices with newspapers held over their heads to ward off the rain, rushed to catch a bus or taxi that would take them home. Among these furtive passersby, Vicente Rosenberg, a thirty-eight-year-old man protected by his hat, was walking calmly but absentmindedly toward Café Tortoni, a fashionable coffeehouse where, in those days, one was as likely to encounter Jorge Luis Borges and the glories of tango as European refugees such as José Ortega y Gasset,

Roger Caillois, or Arthur Rubinstein. Vicente was a young Jew. Or a young Pole. Or a young Argentinian. In fact, on September 13, 1940, Vicente Rosenberg did not yet know quite what he was. As he stepped into the café, he quickly noticed, seated at one of the little tables along the wall opposite the counter, the hulking figure of Ariel Edelsohn, his best friend. He was reading a newspaper as he waited for Vicente, his elbows propped next to his coffee on the marble tabletop, near the billiard tables in the gaming salon. Next to him, gazing toward the back of the café so that he could watch the games, nervous as always, sat Sammy Grunfeld, a young man who often accompanied them. After shaking hands with both men, Vicente had flapped his overcoat to rid it of the last raindrops attempting to seep into the thick wool, then sat down with his friends, tilting his head slightly so that he could read the front-page headlines: in Europe, the Battle of Britain was raging, while the Nazis had begun to segregate Jews and confine them to ghettos. Ariel, whose friends in Argentina called him "The Bear," folded the newspaper and heaved a sigh.

"Jews are a pain in the ass. They've always been a pain in the ass. It was when I realized that my mother was turning out to be as Jewish as her mother that I decided to leave."

"Your mother isn't nearly as infuriating as mine," said Sammy, one eye still on the billiard match.

A little embarrassed, Ariel glanced at Vicente, but since the latter seemed to be thinking about something else, he carried on talking to Sammy, whose back was half-turned to them.

"The worst of it is that, when she was twenty, her great dream was to get out of the shtetl and go live in the big city. She found my grandmother infuriating for the same reasons that I find her annoying now . . ."

"Annoying or not, you still brought her all the way across the Atlantic so she could be by your side."

"Yes . . . we miss even the most infuriating things."

Amused by Ariel's solemn tone, Sammy let out a laugh as brief and booming as the snapping of fingers. For his part, Vicente, who seemed a little sullen, remained silent. For some months now he had had no desire to talk about what was happening in Europe.

"What's the matter with you, Wincenty? Has the good weather put you in a bad mood?"

Vicente turned to Ariel, a half smile playing on his lips: of all the people he knew in Buenos Aires, Ariel, whom he had met in Warsaw when they were both eighteen and both had just enlisted in the army, was the only one who still called him Wincenty.

"My mother is the same, the reason we moved away from Chełm when I was little is because she couldn't stand her parents."

Vicente said the words halfheartedly, and Sammy, whom Vicente and Ariel had met aboard ship in 1920 during the sailing from Bordeaux to Buenos Aires and who, in this still enigmatic city, had clung to them like a lifeline, attempted to bring this casual conversation to a close.

"It's what we've done since the dawn of time, isn't it? We love our parents, then we find them annoying, then we leave . . . Maybe that's what it means to be Jewish . . ."

"Yes . . . or to be human."

After a silence much longer than required by these judgmental words tossed on the table like dead birds, Ariel turned back to Vicente.

"Have you had any news?"

"No, the last letter was at least three months ago. I don't even know whether she received the ten dollars I sent to her in June."

"I talked to Jacob, he's had a telegram from his cousin who managed to get to the United States: apparently, it's impossible to buy stamps in Warsaw these days."

In order not to worry his friends, Vicente forced a little smile then got to his feet and headed to the bathroom. Not that he particularly felt the need to urinate, but for some time now, he had found it difficult taking part in these endless discussions, which, while they began with their past or their families, invariably led his friends onto the slippery political slope of how the situation was unfolding in Europe.

While Sammy and Ariel continued to talk about the war, Vicente, in the vast toilet of Café Tortoni, slowly washed his hands before looking up and glancing at his reflection in the mirror. His features were delicate, almost sylphlike. His lips, his eyebrows, his retroussé nose, his thin mustache (which, regardless of reversals of fortune, he had trimmed twice a week by the finest barber in Buenos Aires) looked as though they had been painted by a Chinese calligrapher with a brush so fine that they were all but evanescent. Indeed, when people thought of his face, it was not the height of his forehead or the prominence of his cheekbones, the green of his eyes, and the russet of his hair that sprang to mind: it was merely a diffuse sensation, like a fine mist, in which caustic humor alternated with tender melancholy.

Having dried his hands, Vicente left the bathroom's chill world of marble and white tiles and returned to the muted ocher world of the café's great room. He sat down next to his friends and gazed at them with affect—and a little twinge of jealousy: unlike Vicente, whose mother and brother were still back in Poland, Sammy had fled the Old World with his whole family, and, three years earlier, in 1937, Ariel had managed to persuade his parents and his sister to join him in Buenos Aires.

". . . in spite of their famous Maginot Line, the French have set a new world record for fastest defeat."

"Well, the fastest besides us, of course!"

"You're different: everyone knows that the Poles never really wanted to fight."

"It's true that Russians like you are always spoiling for a fight, you love fighting . . . especially among yourselves."

Sammy sighed irritably. But Ariel laid a hand on his shoulder like an elder brother and the squabble ended there.

"In any event, our government in exile would have done well to find somewhere better to set themselves up than London. They say bombs are raining down on the city . . . What do you think, Wincenty?"

Since Vicente was slow to reply, Sammy spoke for him:

"London . . . Paris . . . Warsaw . . . We're lucky enough to be here."

To mask his torment, Vicente glanced outside, pretending to check whether it was still raining. Ariel, meanwhile, shot Sammy a look to remind him that Vicente's mother was still in Poland, and Sammy bit his lip to indicate that he had realized his blunder. Around the little table, there was an awkward silence. Then, quickly, to appease his longtime friend, Ariel attempted to change the subject by asking for news of the furniture shop that Vicente had just opened; and, to reassure Ariel, Vicente tried to answer his question; meanwhile, Sammy, in an attempt to ease the tense atmosphere, made a joke about Argentinians' taste for rustic furniture. But despite all their efforts, a glacial wave of silence broke over them, streaming between the looks, between the half smiles, long before they finally stopped speaking.

The three friends had finished their coffees, drunk a gin, and then another, before taking their coats from the hooks and slipping them on and leaving Café Tortoni. They had lingered on the sidewalk for a little while, exchanging innocuous small talk under the awning. Vicente lit up a Commander while Sammy stamped his feet impatiently and Ariel stretched his huge bearlike frame with a groan of satisfaction: these were dark days, but the week was over and he was in decidedly good humor.

"So . . . are you coming with us? After all, it's Friday the thirteenth."

In an attempt to draw his childhood friend into the excitement of the approaching weekend, Ariel had suggested that Vicente come with them to the Palermo racetrack. But Vicente had declined the invitation. Although he liked to bet on the horses, he was tired and wanted to go home. Ariel had not insisted: of the three friends, only Vicente had children, so sometimes it seemed only right to let him go home without a fuss.

Ariel had hugged Vicente, and Sammy had shaken his hand, and they had waited while he finished smoking his cigarette under the awning. Tossing the butt into the distance, Vicente looked up at the sky. Since the rain looked as though it might be stopping, he set off on foot to the apartment on Calle Paraná where he, Rosita, and the children had moved some months earlier. It was a small three-room apartment on the fourth floor of an old building, about a hundred yards from the furniture store that he had just opened. It was barely half past eight, but as Vicente walked through the lobby of the building, he felt a kind of serene joy at the thought that he was heading home, as though he felt, with a renewed intensity, that the modest little apartment that they had moved into only recently so they would be closer to the store was now, and always would be, his true home. "Do you have a home of your own yet? Do you eat dinner at home? And how do you manage with the housekeeping? Tell me everything, my darling. It kills me when I don't have news from you . . ." These words, from an old letter his mother sent back when she still wrote to him care of a Buenos Aires poste restante suddenly came to his mind as he climbed the stairs. "Yes, at last, I can finally say that I have a home," he replied mentally, thinking of her numerous reproaches over the years that he did not write to her often enough. "I am begging you, darling Wincenty, write to me, write to me, write back at once." "I still have no news from you. It saddens me terribly." "I implore you, write a few words to me . . . Is it so difficult to write a few words to your mother?" "All I am asking is a few words. I so long to see you again. For as long as I live, that is my only dream." "I beg you, Wincenty, send me a few lines. You cannot imagine the despair of a mother who has no news from her child!" "How is it possible that a child can completely forget his mother?" When he had left Warsaw, his mother had made him swear that he would write once a week. But, while she had carried on sending him several letters a month until 1938, Vicente had kept his promise only in the first year after he arrived in Buenos Aires. 1929, 1930, 1931. The years passed, and each time Vicente received a letter, he cursed his mother's reproaches. 1932, 1933, 1934. Later, he began to find these same reproaches amusing, and he sometimes made fun of them with Ariel. 1935, 1936, 1937. Later still, he greeted them with indifference. 1938, 1939, 1940. To think that now, for the past three years, it was he who worried because he had no news from his mother . . .

As soon as he stepped across the threshold of the apartment, as though determined to confirm the feeling of serenity their father had felt walking through the lobby, Vicente's daughters, Martha and Ercilia, aged four and six, came running and jumped into his arms.

"Good evening, Captain!"

"Mamá, Mamá! The captain is home!"

Rosita, settled in a new rocking chair made by her father, was reading a story to their son, Juan José, who was still a baby. Having looked up and smiled at her husband, she calmly returned to her page in the book by Horacio Quiroga. So it was Vicente who walked over to the back of the chair, put his arms around her, and kissed her neck. Rosita laid her hand on his and hugged him hard against her shoulder, even as she hugged her son to her heart.

" 'Work . . . We must work in the knowledge that the goal of our efforts—the happiness of all—is infinitely greater than the exhaustion felt by each. This is what men call *ideal*, and they are right. There is no other philosophy in the life of a man, or of a bee.' "

Rosita had finished Quiroga's little children's story and got to her feet. She set her son down on the rug, told her elder daughter to finish her page of writing and her younger daughter to play with her little brother, and went into the kitchen to prepare dinner. Unlike her husband's, Rosita's features were slightly coarse, slightly slack—but so kindhearted. Her eyes and her smile overflowed with a humid, earthy, bucolic gentleness of fertile land. A plump woman, she had a beauty, now so denigrated, that had been much admired from the Renaissance until the nineteenth century: a beauty possessed only by stout women with sloping shoulders, small breasts, and milk-white skin. As Vicente had said to Ariel, carried away by a burst of lyricism the day after he first saw her, "Her expression was so tender that her freckles looked just like tears of joys drifting over her cheeks." Although Rosita and Vicente were very different, in one thing they were terribly alike: both had the hesitant, pale, mute fragility that revealed they had been much loved as children. This resemblance meant that, as a couple, they were both loving and fraternal. In fact, from the moment Rosita's elder brother, Léon, whom Vicente had met at a seedy milonga in a seedy area of Pompeya, invited him to Confitería Ideal, a fashionable tearoom, to meet his sister, Vicente had quickly felt a love so simple and so strong—that is to say, so pure—that he never for a moment doubted that, with her by his side—some months later her father had given him her hand—everything would be effortless and joyful.

And yet at first, Rosita's father, Pini Szapire, had not looked favorably on this Polish suitor only recently arrived in Buenos Aires. "He is too well-dressed to be honest," was what he told his wife on the evening of that sweltering Sunday when Vicente paid his first visit to the family home next to the furniture factory that Pini Szapire had founded thirty years earlier, shortly after arriving in Argentina. But the determination of Rosita, his favorite daughter, to marry prevailed over his reservations. Vicente, moreover, barely noticed the faint disdain with which his future father-in-law initially treated him. A very young officer in the Polish army, he had never completed the law studies he had begun at the University of Warsaw, but, despite his poverty, by the time he arrived in Buenos Aires, he already had a sense of superiority that allowed him to play the dandy with the greatest of ease. Vicente's grandparents had left the shtetl for the city of Chełm, and his parents, in turn, had left Chełm (where his father had made his fortune as a merchant of precious woods) for Warsaw when the boy was twelve. Being born into a wealthy family and growing up in the capital had allowed him to shrug off that inferiority complex he scorned that was common to the children of the Chosen People, and it had given him the courage, at eighteen, shortly after the death of his father, to enlist in the army, where he met Ariel and where he quickly rose in the ranks from a humble private to a young officer.

At the end of the First World War, Poland was scarcely a country. It had five different currencies, nine judicial systems, while multiple border disputes had all degenerated into minor wars: the Polish-Ukrainian War, the Polish-Lithuanian War, and the Polish-Czechoslovak War. As Churchill had predicted, once the war of the giants was over, the war of the pygmies began. Initially, Marshal Piłsudski, of whom Vicente was a fervent admirer, assumed that Poland would fare better with the Bolsheviks than with a restored Russian Empire and, in 1919, ignoring the pressure of the Entente Cordiale to join the offensive against the Soviet Union, he probably saved Lenin's government. But he quickly changed sides and forged an alliance with Ukraine to fight against the Soviets. So it was that in 1920, Piłsudski, who as a general during the First World War had led the Polish legions to their annihilation, was considered by France and Britain to be an unreliable ally who would lead his country to destruction, and seen by Russia as a slave to allied forces bringing imperialism and ruin. Though all agreed that the crowning achievement of his catastrophic career would be the utter collapse of Poland, he won a decisive victory that halted the advance of the Soviet forces through his unconventional strategy during the Battle of Warsaw. In fact, Piłsudski's strategy seemed so naïve, so amateurish, that high-ranking officers and military experts in his own forces pointed out his lack of military knowledge. And when a copy of his plan fell into Soviet hands, General Tukhachevsky himself assumed it was a trap and ignored it. At dawn on August 15, 1920, the armed forces led by First Marshal—now the father of the nation—Józef Piłsudski found a breach in the Soviet front, infiltrated its lines, and slaughtered thousands. The

Soviet advance halted, never to resume. What would later be called the "Miracle on the Vistula" had just taken place.

The Soviets paid bitterly for their mistake: that morning, the Red Army suffered one of the grimmest defeats in its history—and Piłsudski, inadvertently, one might say, became a military genius to rank with Alexander the Great, Julius Caesar, Frederick the Great, Nelson, and Napoleon. It is even said that a young officer attached to the French Mission in Poland, Charles de Gaulle, later adopted many of the lessons from the Polish-Soviet War, and from the career of this capricious statesman . . .

It was in this second war that Vicente had fought. Since his arrival in Argentina, to simplify the account of his earlier exploits, he merely said that he had helped Piłsudski to liberate Poland. He loved to tell the story, especially to make his "big little girl" Ercilia laugh, of how, shortly after he was made captain, when the war seemed all but lost, he took to his heels—and the only military medal he had been awarded was because, of the thousands of soldiers who fled, he had run the fastest. Why did Vicente Rosenberg prefer to belittle rather than boast about his achievements? And why did he decide not to pursue a career as an officer and rise through the ranks of the military? He himself struggled to explain. Neither the battlefield nor his childhood hero, Piłsudski, succeeded in fulfilling the hopes he nurtured in his adolescent heart. And, at the end of the war, he returned, victorious, to a Warsaw in ruins.

His mother, Gustawa Goldwag, immediately persuaded him to apply to study law at the university. Her elder son, Bernard, known to everyone as Berl was just completing his medical degree and, Gustawa, being a good Jewish mother, dreamed of her sons being a doctor and a lawyer. But Vicente dreamed of different horizons, of horizons more distant and more vast than anything offered by an old continent that already heralded calamity. And besides, though he liked to joke about Jews who stayed in the shtetls, and though sometimes felt that he himself was anti-Semitic, he found it difficult to stomach the anti-Semitism of his Polish compatriots. Why should he endure being mocked by unthinking young students on the pretext that they were Polish by birth, when he had fought shoulder to shoulder with Piłsudski to liberate their homeland? Vicente thought about his childhood in Chełm. He remembered the mockery he had endured at school when the schoolmistress asked her pupils to write an essay about what they had done during their vacation, and he had written his in Yiddish rather than Polish. At the time, he was perfectly fluent in both languages, but he did not yet know which he should use at school. And when he had come home in tears, even his big brother, Berl, and his elder sister, Rachel,

had made fun of his mistake. Vicente also remembered
the street where they lived, their neighbors, the district of
Chełm where everyone spoke Yiddish; he remembered that
he, too, once spoke the language that, since he arrived in
Buenos Aires, had become alien to him. Vicente even re-
called the singular feeling he had experienced some years
later, after they moved to Warsaw, when they had a visit by
cousins who lived in Hrubieszów who wore yarmulkes and
sidelocks and dressed all in black: the sense that not only
he himself, but his elder brother, his sister, and his mother
had ceased to be Jews. Since then, in spite of his memories,
this feeling had only deepened. "What is it that makes us
feel one thing rather than another? What is it that sometimes causes us to describe ourselves as Jewish, Argentinian,
Polish, French, British, as lawyers, doctors, teachers, tango
singers, or soccer players? Why is it that sometimes, when
we talk about ourselves, we do so utterly convinced that we
are only one thing, one simple, fixed, unchanging thing,
a thing that we can know and can define using a single
word?" Ever since he left Poland, Vicente, like so many
other exiles, had often asked himself these questions. And
although he sometimes found answers to them—many answers, too many answers!—he never considered that any of
them offered a definitive explanation. Vicente first began
to feel a boundless admiration for Piłsudski of the age

of fifteen, shortly after his father died of a heart attack. Perhaps he enlisted in the army to prove to himself that he was more Polish than Jewish, or more a Pole than a Communist, like his sister's despised fiancé. Perhaps, like so many Polish schoolboys at the end of the First World War, he dreamed of a Poland that was strong and free. And perhaps, too, when Vicente decided to leave Poland, it was because he felt betrayed when Piłsudski, this adoptive father, this hero to a whole generation, abruptly decided to withdraw from political life. Or perhaps it was because of the anti-Semitic abuse to which he was subjected at university. Perhaps he was motivated to leave Europe by the grinding poverty that threatened the entire continent, or by the desire to discover the Americas. Or, more simply, he may have left Warsaw for the same reasons that prompted many others at the time, thinking he would make his fortune abroad and then come home, that he would come home and once again see his mother, his sister, his brother. Perhaps, when he was leaving, it never occurred to him that he would not come back, that he would never see them again.

Whatever his reasons, by 1928, when he and his friend Ariel Edelsohn left Poland for Amsterdam, then Paris, then Bordeaux, where they decided to board the ocean liner that would take them to Buenos Aires, Piłsudski had already reconsidered his decision and embarked on his second political career as leader of Poland, while the anti-Semitic movements within Warsaw universities fell silent for a few short years.

Vicente Rosenberg arrived in Argentina in April 1928 with little money in his pocket and a letter of recommendation from his uncle to the Banco Polaco in Buenos Aires (the same Polish bank where Witold Gombrowicz would work some twenty years later). But, rather than taking a post with the bank, he quickly found himself doing odd jobs here and there, somewhat questionable or shady deals, and became a young man who, if not wealthy, was smartly dressed and gentlemanly; he learned to dance the tango, and began to go to milongas with Ariel and Sammy, and Sammy introduced him to Rosita's elder brother Léon, and Léon introduced him to Rosita, his future wife.

For their part, Rosita's parents had arrived in Buenos Aires in 1905 with her sisters, Olga and Esther, and her brother, Léon. Rosita was the first in the family to be born in Argentina, and quickly became his father's favorite daughter. At the age of eighteen, after she finished high school, she had little trouble persuading him to allow her to continue her studies, and enrolled in the Faculty of Pharmacy of the National University of La Plata. She had just started her sophomore year when Léon first mentioned Vicente to her. At first, she was hesitant to give up everything for this, her first love. She knew that if she abandoned her studies, she would end up becoming a housewife, and she feared this life that, inevitably, would be like those of her mother and her sisters (and thousands of generations of women who had come before her); nonetheless, she gave up everything: even more than becoming a housewife like her mother and sisters, Rosita feared she would miss out on what so many of the novels she had read, and so many of her female friends, called "*el hombre de tu vida*"—the man of your life. And besides, Vicente was not much like her sisters' husbands, or like her own father: Vicente had been to university, he dressed well, and he loved to dance, to converse, to gamble; he made the most of life, as though it had meaning beyond having children and becoming a prosperous merchant.

Rosita came from a family that, though as well-heeled as Vicente (her grandfather, a cigar maker, had had his moment of glory in the 1860s), was relatively unsophisticated and had only left the shtetl near Kiev shortly before she was born. To her, Vicente, like her university studies, offered the prospect of something new, a radical, definitive change that would take her away from the furniture factory where she had grown up.

Her father, Pini Szapire. If he was wary of this young Polish dandy it was not because, despite his elegant suits, he was much poorer than they were but rather because he saw in the young man what Rosita saw in him—and he did not want to lose his favorite daughter, the first ever to express the desire to go to university, the first member of the family who, he hoped, would become "someone" and marry a doctor, a lawyer, or an architect from a good Argentinian family, and not some charming Polish mountebank. But eventually he admitted defeat. Rosita was married and went on honeymoon to Hotel Casino Carrasco in Uruguay. Vicente and Rosita had spent a week moving among the roulette table, the ballroom, and the beach. They spent endless hours dancing, endless hours making love, and endless hours gambling. Vicente was already a passionate aficionado of the green baize, but he hated to lose. And, on nights when Lady Luck did not materialize and they emerged from the casino at dawn, Rosita knew just how to caress him to quickly restore his joy and his smile.

The first years of their marriage passed as quickly as years do when you are happy, when you have three children, when you move house four times, when you change jobs every three months.

In short, in 1940, Vicente and Rosita loved each other as much as ever. Vicente was still young and handsome, he still took great care of his appearance, but he had assented to opening a store selling his father-in-law's furniture, and he had also become a father—and Rosita, for her part, had become a housewife. Vicente had long since forgotten how to speak Yiddish, and learned to speak fluent Argentine Spanish. Apart from his friend Ariel, no one now called him Wincenty: everyone addressed him as Vicente—and at this point, he genuinely felt himself to be more Argentinian than Jewish or Polish.

On that Friday, September 13, after dinner, while Rosita was tidying the kitchen, Vicente put the children to bed. He told them a story he had already told them countless times and which his children, especially his daughters, since his son was still too young to really understand, loved to hear before they went to sleep. It was an old Jewish legend—or a new family legend—which told the story of how he came to be called Rosenberg because of a German poet named E. T. A. Hoffmann. In the days of Napoleon, when the emperor decided to have all Jews added to the civil register, Hoffmann was working as an assessor in the Prussian administration. All Jews had to appear before a tribunal to be given surnames, and the German poet whose role it was to record them, inspired perhaps by the North American peoples, assigned names that were romantic metaphors: Golden Tree, Glow of Dawn, Forest of Diamonds—or Rosenberg, Mountain of Roses.

"But what were we called before that, Captain?"

Vicente had just finished his story that night when, for the first time, Martha asked this question, which was both strange yet utterly logical.

"I think we were called Ben-something-or-other . . . Or maybe not . . . No, I think we took the first name of the father of . . . or of where we were born . . . or maybe the profession we practiced . . . To tell the truth, I don't know. I've completely forgotten."

When Ercilia, pressed him to try to remember, Vicente said that he would ask their grandmother who, as they knew, had stayed behind in Poland; and that if she no longer remembered, she would find other members of the family who were bound to remember. Then he got to his feet and turned out the light.

"I promise, I'll write to her and ask."

Vicente planted a kiss on the foreheads of his daughters, and one on the forehead of his son, who was already asleep, and then left the children's bedroom. Out in the hallway, he turned toward the glow that trickled through the half-open door to the kitchen, but rather than crossing the short distance that separated him from his wife, he leaned back against the wall and stood for a moment, alone in the half-light, thinking. He thought about what he had just told his children. He was a little angry with himself: he knew that he might not be able to keep his promise. Or rather, he knew he could keep his promise about writing to his mother to ask what they had been called before they were named Rosenberg, but he thought it was likely that he would receive no response.

He suspected that she would not write back to him since, for months now, she had not replied to any of his letters.

THE DAY AFTER (NOT THE DAY AFTER THIS FRIDAY, September 13, 1940, when he told his children the story of E. T. A. Hoffmann for the umpteenth time, nor the day after the day after that, nor the day after any particular day, but rather *a* day after, a day as precise as it is vague, or, if you prefer, as certain as it is uncertain), Vicente had left home, walking purposefully. Like any man, that is to say like every man, just as some mornings he got off on the right foot and sometimes on the wrong foot, so the way that Vicente walked differed according to the occasion: thoughtfully, falteringly, furtively, fleetingly, hurriedly—or, as on this day, purposefully. This particular day, this general yet specific day after, what prompted his decision was that he was set to interview a number of candidates who responded to the advertisement he had published in *El Mundo* the day before. When he arrived at his furniture store, Vicente was not surprised to find two young men, one blond, the other dark, and a third, a sullen, bearded older man, waiting outside the door. He raised the metal shutter and first ushered the older man into the long, dark showroom where he displayed his father-in-law's furniture. He had not ushered this man in first because, at first glance, his sullen manner marked him out as a better candidate, but on the contrary, because he was almost certain he would have to rule him out. As indeed he did, when he had finished listening to the man spend ten minutes reeling off the sales positions he had held over the past thirty-five years. As the man himself explained, he had sold almost everything: beauty products, cleaning products, books, watches, livestock supplies, wigs, shoes, jewelry, even automobiles. The man had sold almost everything—except furniture.

"That's just it."

"That's just it? But . . . that's . . . that's just what?"

"We sell furniture, here, that's just it."

The bearded man glanced around the store.

"Yes, I realize that. I can see . . ."

"And so, well, that's just it."

The man had smiled, not particularly reassured. He did not know whether Vicente was joking or whether he was serious. Vicente got to his feet and walked him as far as the door, cutting short the interview to disguise that he himself did not know whether his comment was intended to be funny.

The second candidate he ushered into the store was the dark-haired young man. He was not just dark haired, truth be told: he was very dark. He was very, very dark. He was very, very, very dark in much the way that the other young man was very, very blond. There was something unsettling in the stark contrast between the hair color and complexion of these two men, and, before inviting the dark man in, Vicente could not help but pause for a moment and look searchingly from one candidate to the other. The dark young man also talked about his experience. For the most part he had worked as a waiter in various restaurants, as well as in a gas station, but he felt the desire, as he put it, "to get into a different line of work."

"Are you Argentinian?"

The young man looked at him, a little offended and also a little annoyed: from his accent, it was clear that he was from Spain.

"No, I'm from La Coruña. I arrived in Buenos Aires six months ago. Why?"

"No reason."

Vicente asked whether there was a telephone line at the

place where he was staying, and jotted down the number. Then he walked the young man to the door and told him that he would let him know. Which he knew he would not. Vicente stood for a long time watching as the dark, dark man walked away, turning in surprise at the singular behavior of this improbable store manager, then he invited the very, very blond young man into the store. The very, very blond young man sat down opposite him very, very casually and thanked him with a nod. Vicente studied him in silence: he was dressed to the nines, had thin lips and a thin mustache. In short, although ten or fifteen years his junior, he was like Vicente. And, at first sight, Vicente had decided to engage him as a salesman. He did not quite know why he had made this spontaneous decision, but there was something about him, over and above their resemblance, that he liked enormously.

"Have you ever worked as a salesman?"

The blond young man nodded again, but did not answer. Vicente pressed him:

"Have you ever sold furniture?"

The blond young man gave him a magnificent smile, but still did not utter a word.

"You don't speak Spanish, do you?"

Shyly, the young man shook his head, indicating that the meaning of this last question had not escaped him. Vicente understood, and asked the young man in German whether he had ever sold furniture.

"Never."

"What kind of job did you do before?"

"I have never had a job."

The blond young man once again slashed his magnificent smile. A smile that was utterly disarming.

His name was Franz. And he came from Berne. He and his parents had fled Germany three weeks earlier. And, although he looked to be between twenty-five and thirty, he was only eighteen. Vicente hired him on the spot. The following morning, he started work, which is to say he greeted customers at the front door. From behind his desk, Vicente watched the young man wander up and down outside the store. He had a reassuring feeling now that he was being helped to do nothing very much. And besides, any eventual clients, having done a little window shopping and been seduced by Franz's silent, magnificent smile, came into the shop and, more often than not, left having bought a number of items that more than compensated for the meager salary he had offered the young man and which the young man had accepted eagerly.

Sometimes, as he watched the young man, Vicente wondered why he had hired him, or more precisely, why he had chosen him at first sight. It was only some time later, on the morning of December 9, 1940, when Franz had been working at the store for three weeks, luring customers with his smile, that Vicente was forced for the first time to wonder whether or not the young man was Jewish. Being discreet, he had not dared to pose the question. But on that day, he realized that the moment he first saw him, he had thought: that young man is German. And he had selected him purely for that reason. He realized that he had chosen him for the very reason that, some months later, would cause him to reject anything that could be qualified by that adjective.

A little later in the day on that Monday, December 9, 1940, Ariel had dropped by to take Vicente to lunch at El Imparcial, the oldest restaurant in the city, which stood not far from the furniture store. For the past three weeks, Vicente had not joined them for their regular Friday evenings at Café Tortoni, and, after talking things over with Sammy, Ariel had decided that it was time to see what had got into their friend. As soon as he stepped into the store, having greeted young Franz, who was standing ramrod straight in the doorway, smiling his radiant smile, Ariel noticed that Vicente had a peculiar air about him, as though something obvious yet imperceptible had modified his features: a certain weariness made him seem even more remote and more evanescent than usual. Ariel did not say anything. He wandered around the store, surveyed the new pieces of furniture, and worried about the cost of Vicente's new employee, then they set off on foot to the restaurant, on the corner of Calle Victoria and Calle Salta.

The city center, as always at lunchtime, was clamorous, filled with harried men, street hawkers, and fashionable women popping in and out of boutiques. On the streets, horses drawing garbage carts weaved between automobiles, and despite the sweltering heat, most of the men and the majority of the children were dressed in suits and ties and many, like Ariel and Vicente, wore hats. The great room in El Imparcial was thronged, and the two men were seated in the middle of the room, surrounded by other tables where animated conversations discussed subjects as varied as the previous evening's soccer match (the leading team, Boca Juniors, had beaten their nearest rival, Independiente, five goals to two, and, although there were still two match days left in the championship, thereby ensured they would take the title) and the United States' attempt to negotiate a military defense treaty with South American countries in case of invasion. But the Argentinians mistrusted the Uruguayans, who were wary of the Paraguayans, while the Paraguayans were suspicious of the Chileans, who in turn mistrusted the Argentinians . . . In short, Roosevelt's diplomatic efforts seemed unlikely to succeed.

A ravenous Ariel had grabbed the menu and suggested to

Vicente that they might share a paella, but Vicente was so focused on the political discussion between three businessmen sitting at the table to his right that, without waiting for an answer, Ariel agreed to the suggestions of Gastón, the waiter: a platter of cured ham followed by *arroz negro* for two and a bottle of rioja. Vicente turned away from the businessmen's table and his eyes fell on a newspaper discarded by the lone man taking coffee at the table to his left. He gestured to ask whether he might take it, and quickly thumbed through to the section dealing with international politics. Apart from a piece on the diplomatic efforts of the United States, most of the pages were filled with news about the evolving situation in Greece and in the South Pacific. Anxiously, unable to tear his eyes from the newspaper, Vicente said to his friend:

"You know that I don't often read the newspapers, but you . . . have you heard anything? I mean have you heard anything about what is happening back home?"

"Back home?"

It had been a very long time since Ariel had heard Vicente refer to Poland in such terms.

"Yes, back home," said Vicente with a smile.

Vicente perfectly understood his friend's astonishment, and neither felt the need to clarify a minor misunderstanding that, with a single look, had collapsed beneath the weight of their close friendship.

"Apparently, they've started building a wall in Warsaw . . ."

"Just like in Łódź. They're building barriers everywhere. When it's not a fence, it's barbed wire. And in Warsaw, it is a huge brick wall!"

Ariel read all the newspapers. The Argentinian broadsheets as well as the rare European and American newspapers that managed to reach Buenos Aires, usually several weeks late. He also had connections in the newsrooms of a number of the major dailies, such as *Crítica* and *La Nación*, and a cousin, Alejo Muchnik, who wrote for *La Idea Sionista*, one of the papers serving the Jewish community in Buenos Aires. At the beginning of the summer of 1940 in the southern hemisphere, many people had heard about the anti-Semitic measures being taken by the Nazis to forcibly expel Jews from their homes and confine them to buildings in closed-off zones, about the first convoys sent to the General Government, about the Łódź ghetto, and the wall that was being built to enclose the Jewish quarter in Warsaw, but almost no one in the world knew what life was really like within these ghettos. Though he was both a Jew and a Pole, Vicente, for his part, was less well-informed than most people, including native-born Argentinians who had never set foot in Europe. Of course he knew that Germany had invaded Poland in September 1939. And he was all too aware that, for decades, Germans had nurtured an anti-Semitism as deeply rooted as that of the Poles or the Russians, and one that, since 1933, had become terrifyingly institutionalized. But he had never really come to terms with the dangers faced by his mother and his brother, who were still living in Warsaw, and his sister, who had succeeded in fleeing with her husband to Russia. The wall that the Germans had just built to confine the Jews of Warsaw enclosed an area of barely 1.3 square miles, where four hundred thousand people would be forced to live. Four hundred thousand people in a couple of city blocks; 40 percent of the population of the city imprisoned in 4 percent of its area. One hundred and twenty-eight thousand people per square kilometer. A population density six times greater than that of inner Paris today. Three times greater than that of Dhaka, the most densely populated city in the world.

First, the Germans had forced all Jews living in the various neighborhoods of Warsaw to move to the ghetto. Then came the turn of all the Jews who lived in the surrounding villages. The streets thronged with people, most of whom lived on top of one another. In this teeming hell, one hundred thousand people would die of hypothermia and starvation in the space of two years. One hundred thousand people would die before the deportations to the camps and the mass shootings, before several thousand a day were transported to the camps where the Germans would succeed in turning death into an entirely industrial process.

Before the outbreak of war, Vicente had always refused to read the news from Europe. He had always preferred to avoid the subject. And during the "phony war," between September 1939 and May 1940, he would often say that such news stories were absurd, that the papers were probably "lying a little." Later, though he did not say as much to his friends, he began to think that it served no purpose to know these things, to be informed: what could possibly be done from more than seven thousand miles away? As to the idea of going back to Poland to fight, no thank you. He had been persuaded to fight once before, he had no intention of doing so again. He had fought, he had even succeeded in rising to the rank of captain in the Polish army. But later, at university, he had witnessed the way his compatriots thanked him for liberating their country: with insults, by dismissing him as a "Jew," as though being Jewish meant that he could not be Polish. So what purpose would it serve now, to go back and fight for his people? And what did that mean now, "his people"? In 1940, Vicente might not have been sure whether he was Jewish or Argentinian, but he knew that he was no longer Polish enough to fight, as he had once fought, to defend the country.

"Do you remember Déborah? . . . Of course you do, she was the friend of my sister who married Nathan, the dentist from Poznań. . . . She wrote to my sister to say that their apartment has been requisitioned and twelve of them are now forced to live in one room . . ."

Vicente had listened to his friend recount what little news he had managed to glean about life in the ghetto. Ariel had told him that people feared epidemics, that there was talk of tuberculosis, of typhus, that some people even claimed the Germans had decided to starve the Jews. Vicente had listened to him without saying a word but with immense sadness, a silent despair it had taken some time for Ariel to notice.

"Are you all right, Wincenty?"

Vicente responded with a shrug. They finished the *arroz negro*, they drank coffee, and when they left the restaurant, Ariel once again turned to look at his friend's face.

"Are you sure you are all right? There's nothing I can do? I don't know, you look a little—"

Vicente did not let him finish the sentence. He reassured him with a little nod and headed back to the store. Ariel watched him walk away, wondering whether something had happened, whether there was some particular reason that explained why, over lunch, his friend had been even more taciturn than he had become since the outbreak of war.

Ariel watched Vicente walk slowly away and turn the corner, then, helplessly, he lit a cigarette, turned around, and, still troubled by his friend's mood, set off for home.

For his part, Vicente slowly carried on up the street toward the furniture store. He carried on walking, immersed in his thoughts. Because Ariel had been right: something had indeed happened that Vicente had not mentioned to his friend, something that changed the way he looked at young Franz and had made him even more unforthcoming than he had been before. What was it that Vicente had not confided to his friend? That before he arrived at the store on the morning of Monday, December 9, 1940, an incident had occurred that confirmed the fears he had been feeling for several weeks, the same fears that had kept him from frequenting his friends and Café Tortoni, fears sparked by the rare news broadcasts he chanced to hear on the radio at the café and at the kiosk on the street corner: the postman had handed him a letter sent from Warsaw bearing German stamps and the mark of the Nazi eagle—an envelope on which he had instantly recognized his mother's handwriting.

My darling,

Thank you for the American dollars. You may have heard about the big wall that the Germans have built. Thankfully, Sienna Street is inside the walls, which is fortunate, since otherwise we would have been forced to give up the apartment and move. At least this way, we avoided it being requisitioned. Life is not easy, but we are getting organized. The problem is the crowds. They have brought many Jews from other neighborhoods. They fill the streets with grief. We, at least, can say that we have been lucky. Even if, like everyone, it is difficult for us to find enough to eat. I have had to sell what little jewelry I still had and the fur coat your father gave me on my fortieth birthday. Do you remember? Send us whatever you can. Your big brother sends his love. He would like you to write to him.

Your loving mother.

Vicente immediately wrote back to his mother. In spite of his terrible anxiety, he wrote words he hoped would reassure her. He suggested what he had suggested five years, three years, and even two years earlier, just before the outbreak of war: to come and join him in Argentina. Each time, despite the pogroms in 1935 and 1936, despite the rising anti-Semitism all over Europe, she had refused. She had refused because Berl and Rachel did not want to leave Poland and she did not want to leave them. Vicente knew that his sister would have been impossible to persuade, since she was married to a Communist who believed that, with the Russians, he would change the world. But he felt that his mother could convince his older brother, Berl, who had married a doctor like himself and who had just had a child, to move to Buenos Aires with his family. Vicente could not understand why his mother did not see that the future was here, in the Americas, not in Europe. This time, using more temperate words than he had used back then, Vicente wrote that he knew things were difficult now, but that after the war, he hoped that they would come and join him. She, Berl, his wife, their son, and even Rachel, who was now in Russia. He wrote that he would take care of everything. Everything.

After lunch, Vicente had spent the afternoon in the store. There had been two customers, a man on his own and a couple with their children. Drawn in by Franz's radiant smile, they had bought several items of furniture. From a business standpoint, it was a good day. But Vicente could no longer think of anything except his mother. Details of her face, her hands, the tone of her voice, and certain gestures, like the way she styled her hair, suddenly resurfaced in his memory. He left Franz to close up the store and went home early. He walked slowly, stopping at a café, where he stood at the bar and reread the letter. "Like everyone, it is difficult for us to find enough to eat." Then he continued on his way, clutching the envelope. "I should have insisted.

I should have said it all the time, every week, in every letter. I should never have allowed her to stay in Warsaw." Vicente had arrived in Argentina in 1928, almost thirteen years earlier. He had left Poland for reasons that were complex, various, immense, terrible—reasons that, after reading his mother's letter, now suddenly seemed utterly futile.

When he arrived home, Rosita had just put the children in the bath and started to make dinner. Vicente glanced around the apartment where they had been living for the past few months. Why this little living room with its little sofa looking out onto that little balcony, why this little dining room with its circular table in dark wood and its even darker sideboard, why this little kitchen with its white tiles set off by a frieze of blue tiles, why this narrow corridor opening onto the little children's room and their own little bedroom—why had this insignificant residence become the first place in his whole life that he considered home? Without seeking an answer to this question, without truly realizing that he had even posed it, Vicente turned to his wife, who had emerged from the kitchen and was walking toward him. She looked at him without a word.

"Are you all right?"

Rosita had noticed his strange mood.

"You look . . ."

By way of answer, Vicente gave her a little smile. Rosita

helped him with his jacket and, as she slipped it onto a coat hanger, noticed the letter sticking out of the pocket. Anxiously, she took out the envelope and stared at Gustawa's neat, unmistakable handwriting.

"What does she have to say?"

"Nothing special . . . I'll translate it for you later."

Rosita did not press him. She set the letter down on a shelf and, without a word, took her husband in her arms. Without a word, she hugged him close. Without a word, she kissed his forehead, his eyelids, his cheeks. Then, when the children suddenly began to shriek and call for her, she took him by the hand and led him to the bathroom.

Martha, Ercilia, and Juan José were all sitting in the tub. They had been splashing one another and there was water everywhere. And Juan José had soap in his eyes. Surprised to see their father, the girls abruptly stopped shrieking. Vicente crouched down next to the bath and kissed them; and while Rosita went back to the kitchen to make dinner, he rolled up his sleeves and took care of Juan José.

"What if we went to Las Cuartetas instead of eating at home?"

The water was just about to boil and Rosita, who had already opened a box of ravioli from the pasta factory on the corner, could not help but frown irritably at this suggestion by her husband. But Martha and Ercilia, swaddled in towels, instantly gave a little whoop of joy at the prospect of going out for dinner, and although Juan José, who was cradled in Vicente's arms, did not really understand, his face lit up with such a huge smile when he saw his sisters' excitement that, within seconds, Rosita found she could not help but nod and she smiled too. She helped the children dress while Vicente changed, and fifteen minutes later they trooped out of the building on Calle Paraná.

Night had fallen and the air was finally beginning to cool down. Rosita, Vicente, and the children walked toward Avenida Corrientes, then down through the motley crowd. Haloed by the lamps on the kiosks and the dozens of glowing signs for theaters and bookstores, they strolled toward Las Cuartetas, a pizza restaurant that had opened three years earlier and was now becoming famous. Vicente had his son perched on his shoulders, while Rosita was holding her daughters' hands. As they walked, Vicente gave his wife a brief summary of his mother's letter. And while repeating her words was difficult, he found it helped him, not to forget the sense of the guilt that he would never truly erase from his heart, but at least to recapture the good humor the children had inspired in him as he stepped into the apartment. Rosita reassured him, at least he had had some news, she said, and besides, the war would not last forever and, one day, *ojalá*, Gustawa would be able to come live with them in Buenos Aires. Vicente nodded. He knew that his wife's soothing words masked her reproaches. Some years earlier, Rosita had suggested that if he really wanted his mother to come live with them, he should write to his brother and his sister, or simply go fetch her. But Vicente had done nothing. In fact, he had admitted to her that, since arriving in Argentina, he had realized that exile had made it possible for him to be independent, and that he was no longer sure that he wanted to live with his mother. In 1928, being apart from his mother had been a relief—now being apart from her was torture.

Vicente and Rosita carried on walking and changed the subject. After discussing their elder daughter's school, and the teacher whom Vicente did not think was "up to standard," Rosita told her husband that, as soon as their son was old enough to go to school, she wanted to resume the pharmacy degree she had given up when they married.

"What for? The furniture store is doing well. This afternoon, we sold a sofa and a complete dining set with eight chairs! I am earning enough money . . . I will always earn enough money. You don't need to worry."

"But I'm not worried. I would just like to go back to my studies."

Rosita gazed silently at her husband for a moment, and, seeing his miserable expression, she added in a gentler tone:

"Not immediately, it is not urgent. I'm in no hurry. But, one day . . . one day I would like to . . ."

Rosita did not finish the sentence. It was unnecessary: Vicente understood.

"*Mi Rusita . . .*"

"My little Russian girl." With infinite tenderness, he smiled as he pronounced the pet name he had given her shortly after they first met, merely by changing a single letter of her name. Then, since his wife was already holding both their daughters' hands, he took the other hand of his elder daughter and the five of them walked on, more united than ever. They crossed the vast Avenida 9 de Julio and arrived at the pizzeria. They waited in line with some twenty men in business suits outside the restaurant, and then they waited again at the counter. Before being seated at one of the small marble-topped tables, they ordered a large *musarela*, a small *fugaza*, three portions of *fainá*, a lemonade for the girls to share, and a liter bottle of beer—Quilmes—of which Vicente would drink three quarters. To entertain the children, and although it would be another three weeks before they set off, Vicente started talking about the summer vacation. Instead of going to Mar del Plata with Rosita's parents, as they had done the previous year, Vicente had proposed that they go to Piriápolis, in Uruguay. Both were equally suited to the pleasures of childhood, to games on the beach and numerous activities to keep them entertained through the late afternoons and the evenings; everyone had enthusiastically agreed.

"Damn!"

Vicente had just dripped tomato sauce on his cream-colored tie and his white shirt. Rosita instantly picked up a napkin to wipe it off.

"I mean, honestly . . . What a silly idea, getting all dressed up just to go and eat pizza."

The girls laughed, and Vicente defended himself.

"When you leave the house, you should always be elegantly dressed. Just in case. You never know who you might meet."

As his daughters looked at him in astonishment, Vicente turned to them and explained:

"And besides, it is a mark of respect for all the people you meet that you don't know. It is good to show them you have made an effort for their benefit. It's like having good table manners, you don't just do it for yourself . . ."

Vicente waved his tie and, to make them laugh, he added:

"It's not just so that you don't get your clothes dirty . . . it's for the people who are sitting around the table with you."

The fortuitous arrival of the waiter bearing two bowls of zuppa inglese, the dessert that, together with their pizzas, had customers waiting in line to eat here, put an end to

Vicente's impromptu lesson in decorum—indeed, he was first to joyously break the rules of etiquette, tucking into one of the desserts and gobbling half the bowl, making noises like a pig. In seconds, the whole family had picked up their spoons and were digging into the zuppa inglese, as laughter once again broke out around the table.

Scarcely had he finished his share than Vicente was confiding to his wife how, as soon as the store was "turning a profit," he wanted to find a reliable supplier for New Style pieces so that he did not have to carry on selling only the rustic furniture made by his father-in-law.

"I don't understand. You just told me that sales were better and better."

"Absolutely, and I don't want to stop, but . . . but wouldn't it be good if the store could become . . . how can I put it? . . . somewhat different. We have a perfect location, there is lots of passing custom, and Franz is a great help. I am convinced we could attract a much more sophisticated clientele . . ."

Rosita smiled as she finished the children's zuppa inglese: her father had "opened up" the store to Vicente so that they would have a better life; it was an extraordinary gift, one for which Vicente, being too proud, had never really thanked him. But she also liked the fact that Vicente wanted something different, that he always wanted more than life (or her father) could offer him. This was why she so admired him, this God-given grandeur, this innate ambition about which he never boasted but which inhabited him just as meanness inhabits the skinflint.

"What do you mean we *have to* go to Esther's son's bar mitzvah?"

"Yes, next Sunday. I reminded you about it twice last week."

"Really, are you sure . . . ? Why on earth do we still celebrate these things?"

As they had left the pizzeria and set off back to Calle Paraná, Rosita had reminded her husband of this family obligation that she knew he would think absurd.

"Why do you find it such a strange idea? It's normal to celebrate these things . . . We may be Argentinian now, but we are still a little bit Jewish, don't you think?"

"Jewish?! We don't do anything Jewish anymore . . . Even your parents, despite accents you could cut with a knife, speak to each other in Spanish rather than Yiddish. Even they don't wear a yarmulke anymore! And they've long since forgotten goulash, borscht, and gefilte fish. They eat beef, and pizza and pasta, like us, like all Argentinians!"

Rosita quickly dropped this futile discussion. It often occurred to her that she had married a man who, though born a Jew, had quickly become a Pole, and just as quickly an

Argentinian. And she loved him for this, too. Besides, she knew that she and the children would go to her nephew's bar mitzvah . . . and that there was every chance that, at the last minute, Vicente would decide to go with them.

As Juan José slept soundly in his father's arms and Martha and Ercilia walked happily, hand in hand, Vicente and Rosita carried on talking about everyday affairs and bickering tenderly, like a couple that nothing and no one could ever separate.

THE SUMMER VACATION HAD BEEN A SUCCESS. Vicente, Rosita, and the children had come back from Piriápolis to Buenos Aires and life had resumed its course. Its—what, tranquil? routine? familiar? familial?—course. No, life had resumed its *inevitable* course. Inevitably, Rosita went back to doing the housework, to cooking, to the ironing. Inevitably, the girls had gone back to school. Inevitably, Vicente had gone back to working at the furniture store. Life had inevitably resumed its course—but what else could have happened in Buenos Aires in March 1941, when the news from Europe was increasingly tragic?

In Piriápolis, during January and February, Vicente had begun reading the newspapers assiduously, and the news from Poland finally transformed the love he once had for that country into a deep, bitter, all-pervading hatred that began to eat him up inside and which, while he had not yet admitted it to others, he had already admitted to himself. This hatred he was beginning to feel for Poland and for the Polish people for inexplicable reasons (at the time, Polish Catholics were suffering as much as the Jews under the German occupation). He also felt, more intensely, for Germany and the Germans. Today, it might seem completely natural that a Polish Jew would feel this way. But for Vicente it was not. During his senior year at high school in Warsaw, Vicente had discovered German poetry and loved it. Not simply Goethe, Schiller, Hölderin, Novalis, and Heine, but Mörike, Nikolaus Lenau, and other minor Romantic poets. Indeed, in 1924, he had even considered going to university in Berlin. At twenty-two, his default language, the one that he used every day, was Polish, which he spoke perfectly, without the charming little accent he had had when they first moved from Chełm to Warsaw, but even then, Vicente spoke German better than he spoke Yiddish, his true mother tongue. During his first year at university, his classmates often mocked his passion for German language and literature, and Vicente defended it with a precociously European sensibility: his fascination for Germany was combined with a friendly interest in France, Italy, Spain, England. He could talk for hours about the characteristics of each of these countries, the significance of their respective cultures. Yet, deep down, Poland was his homeland and Germany a potential paradise.

After that heartrending month of March 1941, Vicente would feel a twofold self-hatred: he would hate himself because he had felt Polish, and he would hate himself still more because he had wanted to be German. A twofold self-hatred that could not be assuaged by the fact that he felt Jewish. "Why is it that, before today, I have been a child, an adult, a Pole, a soldier, an officer, a student, a husband, a father, an Argentinian, a furniture salesman, but never a Jew? Why have I never been a Jew in the way that I am today—today when it is all that I am?" Like all Jews, Vicente had believed that he was many things before the Nazis showed him that he was defined by a single thing: being Jewish. In Warsaw, Vicente had been part of the enlightened middle classes who had had enough of being Jewish if being Jewish meant always dressing in black and forever being a little more antiquated than their neighbors. Being Jewish had never really mattered to Vicente. And yet now, suddenly, being Jewish had become the only thing that mattered. "But why am I Jewish? Why, now, is it all that I am? Why can I not be Jewish and carry on being all the things I was before?"

One of the most pernicious things about anti-Semitism is the refusal to allow certain men and certain women to ever cease to think of themselves as Jews, to confine them to this identity against their will—to decide, definitively, that this is what they are. Vicente did not feel as though he had been gifted something, that he had had his mind opened, that he had been enlightened as to what he was or who he was. He did not think: Oh, at least now I know that I am a Jew. Vicente, like many Jews, was merely beginning to understand that, in order to exist, anti-Semitism needs Semites; he was beginning to realize that, if an anti-Semite defines himself as such, he can no longer tolerate that a Semite not define himself, since he is one.

It is not by chance that the problem of defining what exactly it might mean to "be Jewish" had thrown the Nazi administration into turmoil for years. Nor is it by chance that this issue was never completely resolved. Is a non-believing Jew as Jewish as a devout Jew? Is a Jew whose parents or grandparents are not all Jewish truly a Jew? Must we accept the existence of a "third race," or are "partial" Jews, "quarter Jews," and "half and three quarter" Jews as noxious as "whole" Jews? And what of a Jew who does not look Jewish, who does not look sly, does not have black hair or a hooked nose? And what of a Jew who has converted to Christianity, or a Jewish man married to a German woman, or a Jewish woman married to a German man? Nonetheless, being unable to ever truly define this quality—or as an anti-Semite (or a Jew with a sense of humor) would say, this flaw—would not stop the Nazi administration thinking about how to dispossess the Jews, how to later deport them to the camps, and finally how to exterminate them.

Understanding why, at this particular moment in history, German anti-Semites felt the need not only to define the Jews, not only to dispossess them, not only to herd them together, not only to send them to the camps, but to destroy them because they were Jews is not easy. But it is indisputable that the Nazis did not kill Jews because they were Polish, elderly, helpless, blond, married, single, crippled, or because they had bad breath: they killed them because they were Jews. Being a Jew in 1941 had become, thanks to those who sought to exterminate them, the fundamental definition of millions of people who, like Vicente, had never attached any great importance to this classification, to this sense of belonging that was half-religious, half-ethnic, and three quarters who knew what. To be a Jew in 1941 had become a condition that excluded all others, a unique identity: one that defined millions of human beings—and one that would, also, destroy them.

Vicente started going back to Café Tortoni every Friday, and sometimes on Saturdays. As soon as he closed up the store, he would meet up with his friends there. And his conversations with Sammy and Ariel now invariably centered on the very subject that, before the summer, he had tried so hard to avoid: the situation in Europe. In March 1941, one of Ariel's friends, François Martin, a Frenchman living in exile in Buenos Aires who had worked at the French Ministry of Foreign Affairs until President Lebrun appointed Maréchal Pétain to lead the government, had told him about the hare-brained scheme (which he did not realize the Nazis had just abandoned) of sending a million Jews a year to Madagascar. The true aim of the Madagaskar Projekt, a plan devised by the Germans in May and June 1940, was to force a defeated France to relinquish the island of Madagascar so that Germany could rid itself of its Jews by creating an island ghetto, a Jewish reservation governed by the SS, whose inhabitants could serve as hostages to ensure the good behavior of their racial comrades in America. But the way in which the Nazis "sold" this idea to France made it possible to think that they were simply attempting to create a Jewish state, which was how François Martin described it to Ariel.

"In fact, what the Germans want to do is not so different from what your cousin Alejo wants to do in Palestine."

"Yes, Sammy, except that my cousin and his friends at *La Idea Sionista* want us all to move to Palestine so we can live happily together. I'm not sure the Nazis have the same idea . . ."

"Maybe, I don't know . . . Personally, I've no idea what

I'd do in the depths of Africa, especially surrounded by guys like you!"

Ariel smiled at Sammy's words, then pursued his train of thought.

"I'm with you. I wouldn't want to live in a country with nobody except Jews. But that's not the issue. What I meant was that it's a ridiculous idea. It's absurd to try and define us this way. In theory, we're Jews. But in practice, we're not. For some people, the fact that our mothers are Jewish means that we are also Jewish, but that doesn't change the fact that for others, it means nothing at all. I mean, just think about what a preposterous definition it is: if I marry a goy, my children won't be Jewish, but if my goyim sons marry shiksa women, I'll have Jewish grandchildren. Don't you think that absurd?"

As always, Ariel had a clear-cut opinion on the subject.

"So?" said Sammy.

"So, nothing: that's it. And it's appalling. There's something monstrous about the whole notion."

"I don't see what . . . except trying to picture the poor woman who would agree to marry you."

"Very funny . . . What's monstrous is the fact that, if you're the child of a French or an Italian or a Spanish woman that doesn't necessarily make you French or Italian or Spanish, does it? But if you're the child of a Jewish woman, you're Jewish, whether you like it or not."

Sammy had never given much thought to questions of identity. He accepted himself without quite knowing what he was. Ariel, on the other hand, had never been able to tolerate anyone telling him anything about who he was. So the idea of telling him who he essentially was, who he would forever be . . . The three men were standing around one of the billiard tables in the back room. Ariel and Sammy were holding cues while Vicente, leaning against the wall, was smoothing the brim of his hat with a gesture as meticulous as it was monotonous.

"What about you, Wincenty? What do you think about all this?"

"I don't know . . . It's strange, but lately I've been feeling more and more Jewish, even though I don't really know what that means . . ."

Sammy, who had just hit a carom, turned to him, intrigued. Ariel, for his part, looked at Vicente affectionately as he waited for him to finish. But having uttered these enigmatic words, Vicente, as so often recently, fell silent.

"You feel more and more Jewish? What exactly do you mean?"

"You remember Paweł, back in the army?"

Ariel nodded. Vicente turned to Sammy and explained.

"Paweł's mother was Jewish and his father was Christian. And he used to say that it was strange that whenever he was asked if he was Christian, he always said no, and that was the end of it, whereas whenever he was asked if he was Jewish, he always said no, but he felt guilty."

Vicente paused for a moment, as though waiting for his friends to help him clarify his thought. But Sammy simply smiled and walked around the billiard table to line up his next shot, while Ariel lit a cigarette and waited for Vicente to continue. Vicente looked at his friend and then, suddenly animated, as though intoxicated by the phrases forming in his head, began to expand on his theory in a very curious tone.

"It was as though that was the difference. As though being Christian meant being one of a crowd in which no one cares how you feel, whereas being Jewish meant accepting your origins, not so that you could be with others, but so you could be alone and miserable. As though our Jewish heritage is a huge suitcase that we have to carry around all our lives. A huge trunk filled with manuscripts scrawled with illegible handwriting . . . illegible handwriting in a language we don't even speak! As though, because it is not a nationality, because we do not have our own country, being Jewish became . . . became the immense, unwieldy heritage . . . so vast . . . As though by dint of being born in foreign lands, we had to convince ourselves that land was not important, that we were defined by something more powerful—more powerful, but much more painful, something immutable that made our identity inevitable, irrevocable. And yet something that was impossible to share."

Sammy had stopped playing again. Like Ariel, he was staring at Vicente, stunned by the torrent of words pouring out of him. Increasingly frantic, increasingly desperate, almost on the brink of tears, Vicente carried on:

"And this identity, though simultaneously incredible, painful, absurd, and incontestable has something marvelous about it. A people without a country, a way of surviving as though we are truly a nation, but a nation that is not founded on kings, on a single language, on a land that we share or on the wars that we fought together . . . nor even really on a god, since hardly anyone still believes . . . but on a handful of books and a little pile of memories we can barely recall . . ."

"Not to mention the stupid idea that we are chosen, right? On the notion that a god has chosen us for some reason. Even if no one quite knows what it is . . ."

His face still flushed and feverish, Vicente laid both hands on Ariel's arm.

"Yes, yes, that's right! That's exactly right! We are different. We are different from everything and everyone. We are different from anything you care to mention. That is the only thing that matters. We are the only nation without an army, without a state. We were chosen, but we have never really known why we were chosen. We were chosen simply so we would ask ourselves why we were chosen! That's it! We are Jews. I am a Jew. But we don't know what that is. We have absolutely no idea what that means. And the most beautiful thing, the saddest thing, is that we will never cease to ask, and we will never know."

Vicente was staring at his friend. His eyes blazed so brightly that Ariel, worried by this sudden flight of ecstasy, went to calm him. But it was Sammy's brief, resonant laugh that brought him out of this state of nervous exhilaration. Vicente smiled—and regained his composure. He lit a Commander and carried on in a fragile, faltering voice:

"And . . . and I don't know . . . I think . . . these days, I think that . . . that even if it is both beautiful and sad, we can be proud of that."

Vicente released the arm of his longtime friend but Ariel, amused by this sudden feat of oration, slipped his bearlike arm around Vicente's shoulders to keep him close. Sammy looked at them and smiled:

"But, if they manage to send all the Jews to Magadascar, what will become of us? What will make us different . . . ? We'll have a country, and we'll become just like everyone else, won't we?"

"To Ma-da-gascar," Ariel corrected.

"If they do it, we'll have to change. We'll have to learn a different way of being Jewish, the same way we are Polish or Russian. Or Argentinian. The way we are so many things that, fundamentally, don't really amount to much. Things of no importance, things that pass as the seasons pass . . ."

After these more down-to-earth comments, Vicente gave his habitual half smile to encourage Sammy to keep talking.

"I agree with you. Personally, I always felt Russian, I was convinced I was Russian . . . and then, six months after we arrived here, I was just as convinced that I wasn't Russian anymore, I was Argentinian. It's like soccer: when we first arrived and my father had that little apartment out in Nuñez, I supported River Plate. These days, I'm prepared to fight to the death to defend the blue-and-gold of Boca Juniors."

Vicente thanked him with a nod, then turned to Ariel.

"What about you?"

"Yeah, I agree as well. Like you, I could say that I've no idea . . . Jewish? Not Jewish? It depends whether my mother is in earshot! And as for this thing in Madagascar, count me out. It's like parties—it's always more fun to go to the ones you haven't been invited to."

The three friends ordered another three shots of gin, and Ariel and Sammy went back to playing billiards while Vicente finished his cigarette. Ariel missed his shot, and

Sammy made three caroms in a row to win the game. Ariel handed over the thirty pesos they had bet, as he picked up the thread of the conversation.

"In ancient times, when the Greeks and even the Romans were defeated, it was because that was what the gods had decided. Later, whenever Christians lost, it was because their god had abandoned them. But when Jews lose, it's someone else's fault. Other people are always to blame. Everything is always other people's fault. But that's just it—it's as if we've always blamed other people to prove to ourselves that we are unique. That we truly are the chosen people, since we are the only ones who suffer so intensely. And think so intensely! In fact, others resent us, they resent us because they envy us, because they're all jealous of our suffering. They try to humiliate us because we are the most wretched, because we are 'utterly desolate.'"

Vicente shot Ariel an affectionate glance and concluded with these words:

"It's true. Our happiness is the result of abject misery."

Wincenty, my darling Wincenty, my heart, my child,

Everything has become very complicated here. Many of our neighbors in the building have died these past months. Berl treats people for a few złotys, but most of them no longer have the money to pay. We do not know what will become of us. Shlomo still helps us a little from time to time, but even for him things are difficult. The Germans no longer speak to us, they treat us like animals. People are dying of starvation in the streets, and no one even stops to look at the bodies. Looking out the window yesterday, I saw a woman walking up and down the sidewalk. She paced for hours, cradling her dead child in her arms. She sobbed and she screamed and she hugged her dead child and showed it to passersby, to hundreds, to thousands of passersby. And no one saw her. No one. No one saw her dead child. It was as though he did not exist. Fortunately, you are far away from here, my darling Wincenty. And luckily your sister was able to get to Russia.

Your mother, who is thinking about you always.

This letter, posted in the Warsaw Ghetto on September 6, 1941, finally reached Vicente on the morning of October 13. He ran into the postman on his way home from walking his daughters to school, went upstairs, and read the letter while Rosita was ironing the children's clothes and Juan José was playing in his little playpen. When he finished reading it, he stared into the boundless void that extended beyond the walls of their apartment. Rosita quickly noticed his distress and, timidly, as she continued to iron their son's minuscule pajamas, she asked him what his mother had to "say for herself."

"Tell me . . . what has she got to say for herself?"

"What has she got to say for herself?" For a long moment, Vicente gazed at Rosita without a word. Then, unthinkingly, he held out the letter. Rosita gave him a sad little smile and gently reproached him.

"You know that I can't read Polish . . ."

Vicente contemplated his wife. Touched by her gentleness, or her pity, he apologized. Then he told her what his mother's letter said. He told her softly, slowly, as though talking about what the weather would be like tomorrow, or rather what the weather had been like yesterday, something at once unimportant and inescapable. He barely told her that life in Warsaw was more and more difficult. Barely told her that his mother was happy that he was in Buenos Aires and that his sister was in Russia. Barely told her that his mother and his brother were still alive. He barely told her these things. He could barely get the words out: it took an extraordinary effort to put one word after another to form sentences and confide them to his wife.

At the moment when Vicente, with the same extraordinary effort, in the same muted monotone, told her about the screaming woman cradling her dead child in her arms, Rosita stopped ironing and walked over to her husband. Vicente, still seated, had let the envelope slip from his fingers and fall to the floor. Standing next to him, Rosita took his head and pressed it against her belly.

That same day, seven thousand, five hundred miles from Buenos Aires, not far from Königsberg, in the little village of Rastenburg, near Hitler's headquarters Die Wolfsschanze—the Wolf's Lair—Reichsführer Heinrich Himmler was meeting with Higher SS and Police Leader Friedrich-Wilhelm Krüger, of the General Government, and SS-Brigadeführer Odilo Globočnik, head of the police in Lublin. The three men already knew one another, having previously met in Berlin and in Lublin, where Himmler was a frequent visitor. They had already discussed what, at that time, was still called the "territorial solution" to the Jewish question: the idea of deporting all the Jews in Europe, not to Madagascar, but to the East. Krüger had already expressed reservations about the consequences and the technical details, while Globočnik had expressed his enthusiasm about implementing the program. But it was not until today, October 13, 1941, that the three men spent two hours seriously discussing what would be the first institutional and industrialized massacre in human history.

From the inception of Nazism, German bureaucracy had been able to rely on precedents and refer to methods established by Christianity; civil servants had liberally drawn on the vast administrative reserves built up by Church and state. What were these precedents, what were these methods, what were these reserves? In the fifteen hundred years that had passed since Christianity became the state religion, during which an utterly coherent discourse was developed which began by telling Jews: "You have no right to live among us if you remain Jewish," later "You have no right to live among us," and finally "You have no right to live." In January 1939, Hitler first proclaimed his "prophecy" of the annihilation of the Jewish race in Europe. But it was not until the northern summer of 1941 that a series of decisions taken in Berlin would map out the contours of the massacre that would take place over the following four years. In early July, Hitler—convinced, as he told Minister of Propaganda Joseph Goebbels, that "the war in the east was almost won and the Bolsheviks would never recover from the defeats inflicted on them"—ordered the deportation of *all* Jews still in German-occupied territories to labor camps in Poland, then farther east, to the Soviet Union, as soon as victory was achieved. Carried away by the euphoria of his initial victories, Hitler believed that the General Government would be an Aryan paradise. "We have to create a Garden of Eden in the newly won eastern territories." The Nazis had already murdered thousands of Jews and continued to do so. They allowed them to die of hunger and disease in the ghettos, slowly worked those capable of work to death, and put a bullet in those too weak to work as soon as the trains arrived at the camps. But in September 1941, they realized that this method of killing was ill-suited to the coming massacre— the extermination of millions of people. It could not work for two reasons: killing so many Jews in cold blood was beginning to take a psychological toll on soldiers; moreover, the cost of ammunition was too great. Throughout July and into early August, there was still no concrete plan, that is to say, no solid idea of the numbers involved, the timetable, or the location for the killings. In late summer, Obersturmbannführer Adolf Eichmann was summoned to the office of his superior, Reinhard Heydrich, chief of the RSHA, who told him: "The Führer has given the order for the physical destruction of the Jews." But an actual decision on the new method of killing—not simply allowing them to die of starvation and disease, or putting a bullet in their heads, but exterminating them on an industrial scale—was not made until early October. According to Goebbels, making this decision put Hitler in a particularly good mood. These are his words following a meeting with the Führer on October 4: "He is in fine form and his mood is particularly optimistic: he radiates optimism."

Nine days later, in Rastenburg, on October 13, 1941—

the day that Vicente received his mother's letter in far-off Buenos Aires—as leaden fall skies heralded a harsh winter and a dusting of dirty snow covered the rooftops and the cobbled streets, while sipping cognac in a room in one of the castles of the Teutonic Knights, or in one of the dim, wood-paneled restaurants in the city center that smelled of beer, Himmler informed Krüger and Globočnik of Hitler's "historic decision." He explained that the idea that had been germinating in the Führer's mind since early summer—to rid himself definitively of all the Jews—was finally about to be implemented. Himmler knew that Krüger and especially Globočnik, whom he had met with in Lublin on July 20, had been awaiting this decision eagerly. And he smiled and listened as Globočnik immediately outlined plans of a scope and scale that, in his own words, was "considerable," involving the building of a camp equipped with gas chambers in Bełżec. Himmler gave his approval in principal and approved the location for the camp, close to the railway lines and the front-line fortifications whose antitank trenches could be used as mass graves. Two weeks later, Polish laborers began building this camp, the first that would be not simply a concentration camp, but an extermination camp. The decision had been made and was now being implemented: the solution was no longer "territorial," it had become "final."

Vicente, of course, knew nothing of this. He did not

know that the Germans had begun building extermination camps, nor, despite what his mother had written in her
letters, did he know the reality of living conditions in the
Warsaw Ghetto. He did not know that, in the ghetto, Nazis
killed the Jews "simply"—if one can use the word—by allowing epidemics of typhus and tuberculosis to spread, and
residents to starve. Later, he would find out. He would find
out that in late 1941, the daily diet of a Jew living in the
Warsaw Ghetto amounted to 180 calories, or 15 percent of
the minimum needed to survive, just as he would find out
that leaving the ghetto, which some months earlier had war-
ranted a fine of 1,000 złotys and three months in prison, was
now punishable by death.

After telling Rosita what his mother said in the letter,
Vicente fell silent. He briefly accepted her comforting tenderness, then he got to his feet. He took his jacket, took his
hat, and headed to the front door of the apartment. Rosita
followed him and, once again, she took him in her arms.
Once again, Vicente accepted the affectionate gesture.
Then, still without saying a word, he offered his wife a faint
smile, offered his son a faint glance, and left the apartment.
"What are words? What purpose do they serve? Why talk to
her? Why try to explain to her what I cannot even explain
to myself? I would have to tell her the whole story. From the
very beginning. From the day I left Warsaw. Or the day we

left Chełm when I was twelve years old. But how could I say all this? How could I say this now? How could I tell her now when, in all these years, I have never told her anything? Why, until today, did I never feel the need to tell her how passionately I felt about being Polish? How passionately I wanted to be German? Why have I never talked to her about university, about Warsaw, about the shame I felt the first time Polish students mocked me because I was a Jew? Why have I never told her that the shame was more overwhelming than the anger? And why, when I told her that I wanted to save my family, when I told her I wanted to earn enough so that my mother, my brother, and my sister could escape from Poland and come to live with us in Buenos Aires, did I never tell her what they would be escaping? Why did I never tell her how relieved I felt at moving away from my mother, from my big brother, from my big sister? Why did I never tell her that sometimes I longed to save my mother—but sometimes I did not? And what of her, why did she never feel the need to tell me how her mother and her father fled the pogroms? Why, in all our time together, have we never felt the need to talk about the past? How can we have lived together all these years as though the past did not exist? As though only the present and the future were important? And now, now that I should tell her, now that I should talk to the children, now that I should howl with rage and fear, now that I know what is happening there, now that I know I will probably never be able to get my mother and my brother to come to Buenos Aires, now that I know I will save no one, now that everything seems empty and futile, now that there is nothing but a vast abyss stretching out before me, now . . . do I have the right to tell them? Now that I know that it is lethal, do I have the right to ask them to drink some of the venom that is my pain to make myself feel better? Since he'd stepped out into the street, Vicente had felt as though his head might explode. Words whirled and crashed into one another, and if, sometimes, they formed sentences that he could understand, thoughts that he could follow, more often than not they fought and fell, defeated, onto the sidewalk, leaving small blotches as dark as cockroaches that mingled with the pale, greenish droppings of the pigeons. As Vicente walked, as he stared down at these terrible, piti-ful, dead words, he told himself that he desperately needed to stop, needed to stop everything, needed to stop talking, to be silent—that he needed to stop thinking. But even as he thought this, his mind conjured new phrases, sentences that seemed as though they might have another meaning. And he carried on walking, carried on thinking—and once again, all the words became unendurable.

I HEARD FIRULETE IS A NINETY PERCENT CERTAINTY in the third race. I heard it from Chelo, a cousin of Flaco Gomez who works for the O'Neills, and he got it straight from the jockey."

Desperate for Ariel and Sammy's warm friendship, Vicente had started going to Café Tortoni not only on Fridays and Saturdays, but during the week. He would spend hours sitting with them, making the most of their presence, though more often than not he did not say the slightest word.

"Or we could put a bet on Acosta, who's running in the ninth . . . And the odds are three to one . . . Or there's El Pulpo, who's riding in the twelfth, but obviously, with him . . ."

Nervous and garrulous as always, Sammy prattled on

nonstop as he stared at the sports pages of *Crítica*. And while Sammy talked, Ariel stared at Vicente, who was using the tip of his coffee spoon to push a sugar cube around his cup. After receiving his mother's letter, Vicente had spent the weeks that followed waiting for another letter. He waited for another letter with feverish anxiety. He waited for it—and he feared it. He felt terribly regretful that, two, three, five years earlier, he had not been more insistent when he wrote to tell his mother that she needed to come to Buenos Aires, that she needed to persuade his brother, his sister, and their partners that they all needed to come to Buenos Aires.

When he first settled in Argentina, and throughout the 1930s, throughout those bleak years that had seen Europe ravaged by fascism and anti-Semitism, while Vicente sometimes felt relieved that he had succeeded in moving away from his mother, he had also sincerely believed that, if something terrible should happen in Poland, he would be the one to save his family. But something infinitely worse than anything he had imagined was happening now—and there was nothing he could do.

Throughout November and December 1941, and the first six months of the following year—until July 16, 1942, to be precise—Vicente continued to read the newspapers. He read them searching for signs, for clues, for hints that might help him understand what was happening in the country he had considered his homeland. Sometimes the newspapers talked about the mass relocation of peoples, fleetingly mentioned the ghettos, the labor camps, but the information was always vague. Mostly, the information was incomplete, and invariably qualified by "perhaps," "apparently," "probably," and "according to some," which made it possible to imagine something less horrifying than what was actually taking place. The most worrying article had appeared in *La Nación* on February 18, 1942. It reported statements by Anthony Eden that left no doubt as to the fate of Jews in Germany and the Nazi-occupied territories. The British secretary of state for foreign affairs talked about the ghettos, the deportations, the mass killings. But his account was not confirmed by other politicians and observers and was drowned out by the constant and inconsistent uproar of the news cycle.

As with many other readers, the newspapers made it possible for Vicente to know—and not to know. They made it possible for him not to know, for example, that the first operations in the project to exterminate the Jews—little mobile killing squads that followed the German army, exterminating the Jewish population as they advanced—had already begun. They made it possible for him not to know that these "little squads," the Sonderkommandos and the Einsatzkommandos, carried out the "little massacres" all along the Eastern Front: 3,145 Jews here, 8,000 Jews there, 33,760 Jews a little farther on—in total, between one and one and a half million people. The most common method of execution was mass shooting, but they sometimes used a swifter method: all the Jews in a village or a small town were herded into a barn which was then dynamited. And if the German soldiers, having slaughtered all the Jewish men, were reluctant to kill the women and the children, they could rely on the support of local militias, local police forces, and "ethnic" Germans who lived in the area (and whose "passion for slaughter" and "thirst for blood" were such that they "literally appalled" one SS Kommando leader).

This, in summary, is what Vicente Rosenberg could have known, but *could have not known* in late 1941–early 1942. He could have known, but he could not have known from reading the newspapers, which gave only vague accounts of the atrocities that were taking place, the atrocities being committed by thousands upon thousands of men to which thousands and thousands of other men turned a blind eye, refusing to speak of the sheer horror of what was happening. The newspapers made no mention of this horror, and people did not speak of it either. Just as, forty years later, most Argentinians in the city of Buenos Aires refused to believe that the military junta had been responsible for the disappearance of thousands of people, so too, in Germany, Poland, Czechoslovakia, Hungary, Romania, the Baltic countries, in

Crimea, in Ukraine, in Russia, as everywhere in the world, people preferred to say nothing, to know nothing. People everywhere preferred not to speak of this horror for a simple, timeless reason: *because the naked horror of certain events always makes it possible to ignore them initially.*

Vicente's eyes had been rudely opened by his mother's letter. The letter had not completely or definitively opened his eyes, but it had opened them enough for him to make out something that was far beyond anything he had imagined before now, something even more monstrous than was contained in her neat sentences. As he read it, Vicente had felt a nebulous sensation, he intuited faint signs, like unknowable, unutterable words masked by the simple words that made up the text. He had seen and understood things that he could not explain, that he could not put into words— but which would be forever engraved on his mind. Vicente still did not appreciate the horrifying reality of what his mother was forced to endure, what his brother was forced to endure, the conditions they lived in every day, but he knew enough that he could no longer go on living as he had done until now. This was why he had chosen, without yet being fully aware of the fact, to be silent.

"I can understand why he doesn't want to talk about his mother, but why can't he talk about something else? Why is it that every word from his mouth seems to scald him like a drop of molten lava? If he carries on, we'll all forget the sound of his voice. Even Rosita. Even his children. Even me, and I've known him forever." At Café Tortoni, Ariel watched as his childhood friend toyed with the sugar cube. He stared shamelessly. And Vicente ignored his stare with the same shameless lack of discretion. "But what is even stranger is how his eyes have changed. It is as though he can now express anything without moving his lips. Even if he is expressing only his misfortune, he does so with such confidence, such subtlety that it feels as though everything has been said. Yes, his eyes have become more talkative than his lips ever were back when he used to speak. It is as though there is a vast but precisely defined number of things to say, and these things have simply found a new means of expression, a new language that is perfectly suited to them." Ariel gazed at Vicente, who was still pushing the small sugar cube with his little spoon, even as he continued to consider what his friend's life had become. He watched Vicente's glazed eyes contemplate the sugar cube, then something far beyond it, return to the cube, then finally look up into his face or Sammy's face. Ariel watched Vicente's eyes move and realized that these eyes had developed a new perspicacity, an acuity that made them at once utterly precise and utterly inscrutable. Utterly inscrutable, yet tinged with such suffering. "I wouldn't like to be in his shoes. God, I wouldn't want to be in his shoes."

"But if worse comes to worst, we could always put a bet on Romántico in the fifth. Obviously, we don't stand to win much, but, well . . . we have to take what we can get."

"Yes, all right, if you like, why not . . ."

While Ariel occasionally attempted to respond to Sammy, still prattling on, engrossed in the racing pages, Vicente continued to toy with his sugar cube, not listening to the slightest word the young man said. Focused on the desolate void in which he had been living for some time now, Vicente was fascinated by the smooth whiteness of the saucer on which the little cup was placed, by the pearlescent whiteness of the sugar, the mottled whiteness of the marble tabletop. He did not know quite what, but there was something about whiteness in general to which he increasingly felt drawn. His thoughts seemed to vanish, to merge into whiteness, as into the boundless space of another silence.

"Or we can forget about San Isidro and go straight to the bar that Samuel mentioned . . ."

Still pushing the sugar cube, Vicente accidently knocked it onto the floor. And without quite knowing why, this amused him. He smiled, then, without a sound, he carefully set the spoon down on the edge of the saucer and got to his feet.

"I'm just going to . . ."

Vicente did not finish his sentence. Just saying three words required such an effort. Ariel and Sammy watched as he headed to the exit, unconcerned. In the past weeks, they had noticed that Vicente rarely headed straight home when he left the Tortoni. Although he was the only one with a wife and children, he would invariably accompany them, depending on the day, to the racetrack at Palermo or San Isidro, or to play poker.

Yet on this particular day, January 17, 1942, Vicente quickly left the café and headed toward Calle Paraná. Because of an unsuccessful business deal, he had been forced to cancel the summer vacation at the last minute, so, feeling a little guilty about Rosita and the children, who had only managed to get away to Mar del Plata without him for ten days at the beginning of the month, he had decided to go home for dinner.

"Can we have seconds?"

"Can we?"

"Yes, can we? Can we?"

After serving second helpings to the children, Rosita turned to her husband.

"Would you like some more gnocchi, darling?"

Although, as he left Café Tortoni, he felt he missed his wife and children, although he had decided to go straight home so that he could be with them, and although in recent times he very rarely had dinner with them, as soon as he sat down at the table, as always in the past few weeks, Vicente did not utter a word. Day after day, Rosita talked tirelessly to him. Despite his silence, she talked to him as though nothing were the matter, as though everything in their life were normal.

"You don't want any more? Are you sure?"

Finally, Vicente looked up from the void into which he had been gazing and into the void that he could see in his wife's eyes, though they were filled with love and tenderness. Why answer? What difference would it make whether or not he ate more gnocchi? For several months now, he had consented to eat, to breathe, to remain alive. Wasn't that enough? Wasn't that already too much to ask? After a moment, Vicente turned to look at his children. His son, who had just turned four, was chasing the last remaining gnocchi over the white porcelain of his plate. Vicente glanced at him for only an instant before the void once again began to encroach. He glanced at his face, his eyes, then his hand, his fork, the gnocchi on his plate; then, suddenly, a spark inside his brain triggered a series of flashes that made him realize what the whiteness reminded him of. His son's plate, the gnocchi, like the sugar cube, the saucer, and the marble tabletop in Café Tortoni had rekindled the memory of snow, the snows of Poland, the snows of his childhood—the snows that at that very moment probably blanketed the fields around Warsaw, and the mud and the streets of the ghetto where, he hoped, his mother and his brother were still alive.

Vicente turned to his daughters. They had finished eating and, like their mother, were watching and waiting for the eventual, unlikely end of his silence. Vicente's eyes met theirs before returning, without a word, without a sigh, without a smile, to the void that extended beyond the table. His daughters' eyes were also filled with tenderness, with questions, but everywhere he looked Vicente could see only a futile emptiness. "If she was arrested, I just hope they allowed her to keep her shawl. Just that: her pink woolen shawl. That's all I ask, God. That's all I ask, God in whom I never believed. I only ask that if she was arrested, Mamá happened on a German soldier who was human enough to understand that this pink wool shawl could do no harm to anyone." Such futile, fleeting, insignificant details that Vicente clung to on the rare occasions when he allowed his mind to think about the reality his mother might face. "Is she able to wash her hands before eating?" Vicente had never seen his mother eat so much as a crumb without first washing her hands. Now, suddenly, the thought that she might be in one of those labor camps he had recently heard about and could not wash her hands before eating filled him with rage. "No. No no no no no no no. I don't want to. I don't want to think about it. I don't want to think about her. I don't want to think about what she can do, what she can't do. I would rather not think about that. About that or about anything else. No. No, no, and no. I don't want to. I don't want to think anymore. I don't want to think ever again."

"Can I take your plate, Papá?"

"Yes . . ."

Vicente spoke and saw his elder daughter smile at him. She was smiling at him with infinite gentleness but he, being completely distracted, had answered instinctively without truly understanding the question. He had answered with a completely distracted "yes," a "yes" that meant nothing at all.

"Yes. I'm sorry, darling. Yes, of course you can."

Brought back to the present by her smile, he pulled himself together and eventually managed to pronounce these few words. Ercilia smiled again.

"Thank you, Captain!"

She picked up his dirty plate but, rather than allowing her to take it into the kitchen, he gently took her wrist and sat her down on his knee. Ercilia set down the plate again and rested her head against his shoulder; and there they stayed, in silence, pressed against each other in the deserted dining room.

Three days later, on January 20, 1942, in a quiet villa set on extensive grounds in a fashionable southwestern suburb of Berlin, only a few miles from the city center, the famous Wannsee Conference was held. Fifteen of the most senior officials in the Third Reich were gathered to discuss the bureaucratic, technical, and economic practicalities of the "final solution to the Jewish question" requested by Hitler. In order to carry out such a vast industrial project, Reichsmarschall Hermann Göring, Himmler, Heydrich, and Eichmann would require resources, materials, and manpower that the Reich was already devoting to a very different logistical challenge—the war. And it was chiefly in order to prevent certain elements within the government (the ministries, the tribunals, the armed forces) from creating obstacles or refusing to cooperate that it was decided to invite the leaders of all the departments concerned to this meeting where the project and the means for its execution could be explained. Heydrich opened the conference by reminding those present of the anti-Semitic measures adopted by Hitler since the Nazis came to power, commending the fact that the period from 1933 to 1941 had seen the expulsion of some 537,000 Jews from Germany and Austria. "Unfortunately," according to his figures, there were still approximately 11 million Jews living in Europe and the French colonial empire. Heydrich's presentation lasted for almost an hour. There was talk of the logistical and organizational details relating to the fate of these Jews, who, according to the text of the conference protocol, were to be "evacuated" to the East, where they would be "treated accordingly." The goal—which, according to the testimony given by Eichmann at his trial twenty years later, had been discussed openly over a glass of cognac after the conference, so that all of the attendees were clear—was that, once the undertaking had been completed, there would no longer be a Jewish problem to be solved: a small number of Jews were to be used for work related to the war effort while the rest, the vast majority, were to be killed in extermination camps.

Eleven million people. Eleven million people to be killed. Is it possible to think the unthinkable? Is it possible to imagine something no one has ever seen, something no one has ever imagined mankind was capable of doing? From time to time, events occur that change what we are capable of imagining, that push the realms of possibility to limits that were previously inconceivable.

Until the summer of 1942, however, the decisions taken at Wannsee could not be implemented. On the one hand, since the extermination camps were not fully functional, the Reich continued to herd Jews into the ghettos while waiting for the camps to be opened. On the other hand, after the enthusiasm of October 1941 that greeted the dazzling advances of the Wehrmacht, the German defeat at Moscow in December had led to a comprehensive review of priorities: the euphoria kindled by the prospect of a swift victory had given way to the prospect of a protracted conflict and the realization that there were insufficient food supplies to feed the people of Germany and the occupied territories. The Nazis therefore decided to deport all European Jews to the East, though they could not immediately kill as many as they had hoped. In fact, from the fall of 1941 to the spring of 1942, the lives of millions of Jews would depend on how the Germans daily resolved the delicate balance between killing them so that they did not eat the food needed to continue the war effort and allowing them to live so that they could make the weapons needed for the war effort. But this uncertainty about how to deal with the Jews—kill them immediately or kill them after making them work—would not prevent the death toll from rising into the millions. In Lublin, the district run by Odilo Globočnik, about a million deported Jews would be deemed unfit for work and murdered as soon as they arrived in the camps.

Did Vicente sense the terrible immensity of what was happening in Europe? Did he have any real understanding of what threatened his mother and his brother beyond a miserable life and a miserable death in the ghetto? No. In spite of his mother's letters, like most Jews in the world, Vicente could not have imagined what he would later discover. He could not have inferred that thousands of people were being killed every day, that thousands of people were being murdered every day, shot in the head or led into the gas chambers, that thousands of corpses were burned in ovens whose flames licked the heavens.

Since he began to get a glimpse of what was happening in Europe, Vicente had felt increasingly Jewish. But that was not always enough to reassure him. Before 1939, Vicente had often asked himself whether he was this or that, Argentinian or Polish, Jewish or atheist. And he had salved—or pricked—his conscience with the thought that not knowing what he had in common with himself, with the man he had been yesterday, with the man he would be tomorrow, with who he was when he was beside himself with joy or the man he was when he was beside himself with rage, with who he had been as a child or who he would be when he became a grandfather, how could he know what he had in common with some random Argentinian or some random Jew about whom he knew absolutely nothing? "Man is so insignificant that he does not know the taste of his own flesh or the day that he will die. Why ask him to give a simple, succinct response to the questions posed by the shifting and mysterious thing we call identity?" This is what Vicente had often thought in the past. Now such complex thoughts no longer formed in his mind. Now he simply felt more and more Jewish—though it afforded him no relief whatsoever.

Franz, the young German sales assistant Vicente had hired in early December 1940, took more and more responsibility for the store, which he managed better and better. He taught Vicente how to charm the customers, to handle the accounts, and to manage the stock. And during the long months when they worked together, Vicente had come to know him. One evening as he was closing up the store, some weeks before he received the letter from his mother, Franz let slip that it was his birthday and Vicente invited him for a beer. They had walked down toward the river and stopped at a bar on Calle Florida. They drank the first Quilmes in silence, watching the passing pedestrians. Vicente felt calm. And he enjoyed sharing his silence with Franz. He liked to look at him, liked to look at his dazzling smile. Often, it was enough to alleviate his misery. Franz, as always, seemed to be contemplating the whole universe with an intense joy.

"This is one of the things I like most about Buenos Aires: sitting on a café terrace and watching the people pass by."

Vicente glanced at him knowingly.

"The people?"

Franz's smile grew broader, spilling over from his lips to his cheeks, his eyes.

"All right, the girls. Especially the girls."

Vicente gestured to the waiter to bring them another bottle of Quilmes.

"I'll get this one . . ."

"Don't worry, you can let your boss pay for a beer."

"You're not just my boss," Franz said, blushing a little. "You're almost like a father to me."

"A father?"

"Yes, well . . . a mentor . . . I don't know . . . a spiritual father."

Franz and Vicente exchanged a look—whether knowing or unknowing, like a silent question and a vain answer—then they turned back to the street, raising their glasses at precisely the same time and taking a sip of beer.

"Speaking to me in German, even though I'd only just arrived, even though you knew nothing about me, giving me a job when I didn't speak a word of Spanish, all these things felt like you were saying that I could find my place in this country I barely knew. I've never known why, that first day, you spoke to me in German so candidly, so directly . . ."

"I could just tell that you were not a native and I imagined . . . I don't know what I imagined . . ."

"You could have spoken to me in Polish . . . or in Yiddish . . ."

"Yes, that's true . . . but . . ."

His heart suddenly swelled by rage and shame, Vicente lowered his eyes as he finished the sentence:

". . . I've always loved German."

Understanding his pain, Franz fell silent for a moment and wiped the magnificent smile from his face.

"Once, a long time ago, you asked me if I was Jewish. But you never asked me why my parents and I left Germany."

Vicente turned to the young man again, expectantly.

"We left Germany because my parents are Communists. And so am I."

Vicente could not help but give a little expression of surprise—and disappointment.

"Actually, back in Germany, I was too young to be involved in politics, but I've always subscribed to the ideas of Lenin. And of Trotsky in particular."

Vicente, who was beginning to be irritated by this change in the conversation, turned back to look at the street.

"What? What's the problem with Bolsheviks?"

"Nothing."

To avoid telling Franz that, twenty years earlier, he had feared, he had hated them, he had waged war against them, Vicente drained his glass. Franz waited for him to expand on his response, but Vicente simply poured himself more beer and looked at him in silence: Why should he confess all this when he no longer felt the slightest fear and could not possibly hate his young employee? Fortunately, some friends of Franz's, a boy and two girls about his age, happened to be passing and stopped at the table, putting an end to the conversation.

In fact, over the months, Vicente had grown increasingly close to this cultured young man with whom he often talked about poetry. He had become increasing fond of young Franz until the moment when, some weeks after receiving his mother's letter, he found he could not bear his presence and had dismissed him on some trivial pretext. Franz did not complain: despite his genuine affection for his boss, Vicente's silence and unendurable melancholy had begun to outweigh his desire to work and to learn. Franz had left and Vicente once again found himself alone in the dark, narrow store.

Summer gave way to fall, fall to winter. Vicente carried on working, visiting Café Tortoni, and sometimes, increasingly silently, looking after his children. And sometimes, increasingly silently, making love to his wife. Meanwhile, in Europe, Paris was enduring the first bombing raids by the Royal Air Force, the Wehrmacht had taken Sebastopol, and Reinhard Heydrich died—finally—from sepsis contracted from shrapnel wounds sustained in the assassination attempt that had failed to kill him a week earlier.

On Thursday, July 16, 1942, the same day that police officers and gendarmes in Paris rounded up thirteen thousand Jews (including some four thousand children) to deport them to Auschwitz, Ariel braved the torrential Argentinian rain to drag his bearlike carcass as far as Vicente's furniture store. He came to show him a copy of a British newspaper printed three weeks earlier that had only now arrived in Buenos Aires. While the German advance had begun to falter and the war had become gradually more unsettled, *The*

Daily Telegraph, a right-wing London newspaper, had published what might be considered one of the greatest scoops in history. The headline ran: GERMANS MURDER 700,000 JEWS IN POLAND. The subheading: TRAVELLING GAS CHAMBERS.

"More than 700,000 Polish Jews have been massacred by the Germans in the greatest massacre in the world's history. In addition, a system of starvation is being carried out in which the number of deaths, on the admission of the Germans themselves, bids fair to be almost as large. The most gruesome details of mass killing, even to the use of poison gas, are revealed in a report sent secretly to Mr. S. Zygielbojm, Jewish Representative on the Polish National Council in London . . ."

This incredible scoop took up two columns on page 5 of a newspaper that ran to only six pages. The least that can be said is that its publication, at the time, provoked little comment: the story was not picked up by other newspapers, and was barely mentioned by public figures or politicians. Indeed, Szmul Zygielbojm was accused of making the whole thing up.

"Children in orphanages, pensioners in almshouses, and the sick in hospitals have been shot." "Men and boys between 14 and 80 have been driven together into one area, usually a public square or a cemetery, and there killed, either by knifing, machine-guns, or grenades. They had to dig their own graves beforehand."

The details were horrifying. Vicente began reading with the same skepticism he generally brought to reading newspapers, but by the end, he felt a pang of anguish and a knot in the pit of his stomach. As soon as he had finished reading, he gave the paper back to his friend. Ariel had expected a reaction, but Vicente said nothing. Ariel tried to talk to him, tried to get him to discuss these atrocities, tried to share his feelings of helplessness, bitterness, and anger with his friend—and he also tried to persuade Vicente that, for as long as he had no news of his mother and his brother, hope was still possible. He even said—absurdly—that, after all, the unimaginable number of 700,000 victims represented only one third of all Polish Jews.

Vicente listened to him coldly, without uttering a word. Needless to say, Ariel quickly realized his blunder, his mistake, but even then, he pressed on. He persisted and persisted; he rephrased his clumsy words, and added many others, filled with rage and compassion; he tried every means possible to share his grief with Vicente, then, not knowing what to do, feeling miserable and furious and deeply wounded by his friend's glacial, taciturn reaction, he finally hugged him and left the store, with fists clenched and tears in his eyes.

Vicente sat alone for a long moment, then got to his feet

and went to the door. He calmly turned over the sign to indicate that the store was now closed, then crept over to a gramophone he had put on sale only a few days earlier. He placed a record on the turntable and settled himself in an armchair.

And, as the first chords of Mozart's Piano Concerto no. 24 rang out, he closed his eyes.

I N FACT, THE REALITY IN EUROPE IN JULY 1942 WAS
worse than what had been described in the *Daily Tele-graph* article. The mobile gas chambers (the first generation, disguised as small trucks from a company called Kaisers-Kaffee, and the second generation, 2.5- and 3-ton trucks that held between thirty and fifty people, and the 5-ton trucks that could fit as many as eighty victims—*standing and tightly packed*—fitted with special hermetic chambers into which exhaust fumes were directly funneled) had already been replaced by the fixed gas chambers that, since March and April, had been operating in the extermination camps of Bełżec, Chełmno, and Auschwitz. And, on July 19, 1942, the day of Vicente's elder daughter's eighth birthday, Himmler signed the order to set in motion Aktion Reinhard, with the

stated goal that, from December 31, 1942, no persons of Jewish origin would remain within the General Government.

In Warsaw, the Germans began by offering bread and jam to those in the ghetto who agreed to be evacuated to labor camps, and many thousands responded to the call. Then, over the summer of 1942, they began calling for the "resettlement to the East"—which, in practice, meant the deportation of all Jews from the ghetto to the extermination camp Treblinka II. This ancillary operation, code-named the *Großaktion* (Great Action), began on July 22. In the space of eight weeks, some seven thousand people were deported daily. People were snatched from the ghetto day and night, from the streets and from their houses. Jews were taken to the Warsaw *Umschlagplatz* and, from there, by train to Treblinka, fifty miles away, which, they were told, was a transit station from which, having been disinfected, they would be transferred to labor camps farther east. The road that led to the "showers"—which more than 300,000 Jews from the Warsaw Ghetto would take over the summer of 1942, and more than 450,000 Jews from Radom, Lublin, and Białystok would take in the months that followed—was dubbed by Nazis the *Himmelstrasse*: the "road to heaven."

July, August 1942. Meanwhile, in Buenos Aires, the changeable weeks of winter in the southern hemisphere flashed past and Vicente still had no news of his mother.

Night after night, he stayed up until dawn playing poker and never woke before two or three o'clock in the afternoon. He would emerge from the bedroom, go into the bathroom to splash water on his face, have a quick cup of coffee, give his children a half-hearted kiss as they came home from school, then head to the store to see whether the new salesman he had hired, a Greek man of about fifty named Yorgos, had sold anything. In order not to think about his mother, Vicente also forced himself not to think about Rosita, or the children, or himself. The slightest compassion for another human being seemed like an insult to . . . to what, exactly? To his mother's circumstances? To her suffering? To her memory?

"Say nothing. Yes, say nothing. Forget what it means to speak. What it means to mean. What a word denotes, what a name names. Forget that words, now and then, form sentences." Silence, he hoped, like gambling, would help allay his torment. He longed for a silence so powerful, so constant, so insistent, so relentless that all things would become remote, invisible, inaudible—a silence so deep-rooted that everything would be lost in a blizzard of snow. Vicente wanted to silence the voices of others, the voices around him, and his own voice too. Or, rather, he wanted to silence his *voices*: the one that, albeit rarely, still uttered words that others could hear, and also the other voice, the mute, internal voice that spoke to him more and more often, at times sounding like a close friend and at times like an alien god—the voice of his conscience. He wanted to silence everything. He longed for everything to forever be as silent as a vast steppe blanketed by snow. And often, by dint of sheer perseverance and stubbornness, he managed to succeed. He would be silent for long hours during which no voice from the outside world would reach him, no thought would express itself within his mind. Music was a great help: the *St. Matthew Passion*, the Mozart piano concerti, and, above all, the lighter works of Beethoven: *Für Elise*, the *Moonlight Sonata*, the *Bagatelles*, the *Variations*. "Germans. Three Germans. Although Mozart . . . but he apparently considered himself German." At the store, Vicente listened to certain pieces over and over to silence the world and his memories, and to blot out the slightest image conjured by his imagination. But after some weeks, even music was no longer necessary. The silence he imposed upon himself was such that he could spend endless hours when the only thoughts to pass through his mind were considerations of trivial importance; or, in the evening, after Yorgos had left, he would sit at the back of the store, he would watch pedestrians stroll past the window; to say nothing of the other hours, just as endless, when, sitting at the poker table, he would lose what little money he had left. "No more words. No more languages. Neither German, nor Polish, nor Yiddish. Nor Spanish, nor Argentine. No more words. No more names. No more names for anything. No word for music, for piano, for chair, for table. No word for window, or store, or street, or motorcar, or horse, or city, or country, or ocean. Or massacre. Or suffering. No. More. Words."

Rosita coped with this new way of living as best she could. She found the time increasingly long, but she busied herself with the housework, the meals, the children, and ironed her husband's shirts as conscientiously as she had always done. Sometimes, as on this Sunday afternoon in mid-August, she would watch him come and go immured in his self-imposed silence. She would watch as he did nothing, said nothing, and ask herself why he was no longer the man she had married. Not knowing what monsters were stirring inside his mind, wondering what she had done, in what way she was to blame. "I love him. I love him I love him I love him I don't love him but I love him. I love him. I don't love him. I love him. But why? Why has he stopped shaving as he used to? Why does he look so shabby and unkempt? Why has he stopped taking pride in his appearance? And why does he no longer take care of the children? Even silently? It is not difficult to walk them to school as he used to do, to collect them from time to time . . . Why? Why why why? Why is he no longer the man he was when

I first met him? When he married me? When he loved me? When I loved him? I don't know who he is anymore. That is the problem. No more, no less. I don't know. I don't know anymore. Sometimes he looks at me, sometimes he smiles at me, but I don't know. I love him. I love him I love him I love him. But I don't love him. Do I even know, could I even say what it is that I still love about this man I loved so much, this man who was, who should forever have remained, the love of my life?" Rosita asked herself many questions, but could find no answers. She thought about her husband, and she thought, too, about her parents, about their suffering. "They, too, faced horrors, like Gustawa. They, too, witnessed terrible atrocities. How did they cope then? And how have they managed to forget? How, when they arrived in Argentina, did they manage to forget the pogroms? How did they manage to put the past behind them and begin to live again? What did they part with? What did they erase? What did they abandon? What did they give up so that I, and my brother and my sisters, could live a normal life?" Rosita had chosen to marry Vicente. She had chosen to give up her studies to become his wife. No one had forced her. Yet was she any happier than her sisters, or her mother, whose marriage had been an arrangement between her parents and the parents of a boy from a neighboring shtetl? "I cannot love him. How can I love a man who is no longer present? Who is not here even when he *is* here? I have no idea what he is thinking, what he is feeling, I have no idea what he wants. The last time I touched his hand, it was as cold as a dead man's."

On this Sunday afternoon, like so many others, Rosita had watched her husband skulk around the apartment, without a word, without a glance for her, for their daughters busy doing their homework at the dining table. Later he had sat on the sofa and gazed through the window at the sky. Vicente now lived in a world in which his wife and children scarcely existed. At some point, in the children's bedroom, Juan José woke up from his nap and started to cry. Rosita, in the kitchen, had just started to wash the dishes. Deliberately, she waited for several long minutes. She wondered whether her husband could hear his son's wails. She wanted to know whether he would get up and tend to their son. But she waited—and he did nothing. And it was she who had to leave the dishes and go to take Juan José in her arms.

As almost every day for weeks and weeks now, Vicente felt exhausted. Today, since it was Sunday, he had had woken a little earlier than usual, left the apartment, and spent much of the day walking, walking aimlessly, as he was increasingly wont to do, wandering like a lost soul through the streets of Buenos Aires. The city streets were filled with motorcars, lined with kiosks, boutiques, bookstores. And women, women who were increasingly beautiful, or rather increasingly attractive, increasingly elegant. The opulence bestowed upon this far-flung country buried in the depths of South America by a war waged half a world away seemed to have transformed many of the streets of Buenos Aires into catwalks for fashion shows. Vicente had loved this city. He had loved to stroll, to explore its streets. He had loved to stray from the center into the louche, even dangerous neighborhoods of Boedo, Barracas, or Pompeya, just as he loved to meander through Recoleta, Palermo, and Belgrano, the chic districts that flanked the river to the north. Between the day he arrived in Buenos Aires in April 1928 and this winter of 1942, the streets of the city had filled with life, with bustle. Argentina had recaptured the opulence it knew in the 1910s. No longer the poor, insignificant country it had been in the aftermath of the crisis of 1930, it had become what the Second World War had made of it: a distant center of the world. The war that now ravaged Europe had prompted a huge increase in immigration, bringing not only the poor Spaniards and Italians who had been drawn to its shores since the nineteenth century, but celebrated artists and intellectuals, and European families considerably wealthier than those who had come before them. For Argentinians, life was easy. The stores were filled with merchandise, every business venture prospered. In this vast metropolis, this bustling city, only Vicente felt increasingly poor, increasingly destitute.

Before the war, eager to be more of a *porteño* than any Argentinian in the city, Vicente loved to roam these same streets he still walked today. He loved to weave and zigzag, determined to know every little alley. He would walk for hours and hours, gazing at storefronts and at passersby. Now, however, though he sometimes walked as far as Chacarita or La Boca, he took a single street and walked in a straight line, as though he had no control over where his feet might lead, as though it did not matter. He walked endlessly, staring at his feet. Then he turned back, taking the same street home. Since receiving his mother's letter, Vicente had spent hours walking though he took no pleasure in walking. But, since he took no greater pleasure in not walking than in walking, aimlessly, inexorably, he carried on walking.

Walking alone has always afforded men the chance to be silent—and to think. Yet Vicente walked only so that silence could dog his footsteps. As previously, when he still listened to music, or sat on the sofa staring through the window at the sky, when he walked, he longed for words to fade so completely that thought itself disappeared. But, unfortunately, though stillness is the opposite of motion, though silence is the opposite of speech, there is no opposite to thought, nothing that counters the workings of the mind: not thinking is merely another form of thinking. "What about Berl? Is he still working? Is he still fighting? Or has he given up too? How could my brother, my older brother, so tall, so strong, so self-assured, have been reduced to one of the miserable wretches they talk about in the newspapers? Have the Germans crushed and humiliated him? Have they turned him into a servile animal?" And so, as he walked, having spent long minutes struggling with his inability to not think, Vicente's thoughts invariably came back to himself and to the demons that plagued him at that time.

In spite of his mother's letter, in spite of the *Daily Telegraph* article, Vicente had only the most nebulous idea of what was truly happening in Europe. All around the world, newspapers had timidly begun to speak of the hundreds of thousands of Jews murdered by the Nazis. But, since it is impossible to imagine the murder of hundreds of thousands of human beings, most people still did not believe it. After the *Daily Telegraph* article in July, two Argentinian newspapers, *La Prensa* and *Crítica*, had published stories alleging that the Jews were being deported to extermination camps. Then, on November 25, 1942, the *New York Times* published an article about the camps at Bełżec, Sobibor, and Treblinka, and the gas chambers and the crematoriums in Auschwitz. The article explicitly reported on the massacres of elderly Jews, as well as all children between the ages of one and twelve, and all those unfit for work. But the brief article appeared on page 10 of the newspaper, and, once again, was not taken up by other newspapers.

Vicente, like the rest of humanity, could have known but could *not have* known. He could not put an image to what was taking place eight thousand miles away from where his own tragedy was being played out. He had no image for it, nor did he have a word for it. Indeed, it is astonishing how difficult it was, not just for Vicente, but for the world at large to name what was happening. In the beginning, it was not referred to as the Shoah or the Holocaust. Either in French or English, either with or without capital letters. In the beginning, it went unnamed. People talked about the "event," about a "catastrophe," a "cataclysm," a "disaster," later there was talk of "hecatombs," of "apocalypse." But in the very beginning it had no name. Except among the Nazis, who initially called it the "territorial solution" and later the "final solution," and these names in turn were cloaked in veiled terms (the gas chambers were referred to as *Spezialeinrichtungen*, "special equipment," gassing as *Sonderbehandlung*, "special treatment"); as a result, outside the vocabulary of the executioners, for many years what was happening in Europe went unnamed. Or, as Churchill said, "a crime without a name." Later, after the war, there was much discussion about what to name this event. Much discussion, because to name something is invariably a way of saying something that has not been said and, at the same time, to say something that has always been said—or has always gone unsaid, which amounts to the same thing.

After the Wannsee Conference, the Nazis began to talk about the "final solution," and, bizarrely, this euphemism continued to be used by everyone for decades, as though Westerners at the time knew the very thing that they deny today—that they were all guilty. "The final solution." Such a strange expression, isn't it? A solution, as we know, invariably raises other questions, other problems. Not this one. The countrymen of Kant, Hegel, Schopenhauer, and Nietzsche believed that this solution, this *final* solution would resolve everything.

Later, the preferred term became *genocide*, a word composed of the Greek *genos*, meaning a group from the same origin, and the Latin suffix -*cide*, from the verb *caedere*, to strike down, fell, slay. Coined by a Polish Jew in 1944 and adopted by the United Nations after the Second World War, the term was never exclusively reserved for the extermination of the Jewish people—which discouraged its use by those who believed the Shoah was a unique event in human history.

A little later, Anglophones tried using the term *Holocaust*. But *holocaust* has always referred to a sacrifice, a burnt sacrifice offered to the gods. It has always denoted the action of making a burnt offering to the gods. For millennia, humans have burned animals and offered the best of them—the smoke, the fragrance—to their gods. And, in return, they have asked things of those gods. Did whoever first used the word *Holocaust* to refer to the slaughter of the Jews have this sense in mind? We will probably never know. But words do not rely on what a speaker believes them to mean: words express what they become, they always tell a story, *many* stories. Whoever first chose the word *Holocaust* was saying, wittingly or unwittingly, that the murder of millions of Jews was a sacrifice made to certain gods as a petition for certain things. Let us hope that this man was speaking of his gods. Or rather, let us hope that this hypothetical man suggested the word because he realized that God was dead, because he had seen God forever dispersed in the smoke from the human holocaust demanded by race, the most voracious of all idols.

After *Holocaust*, or perhaps before (since it has been used since the Talmudic period to designate the destruction of Jerusalem and the sack of the First and Second Temples), there was also the word *ḥurbān*, whose choice was motivated by the desire to include this event in the continuum of catastrophes and destructions suffered by the Jews.

Then eventually, from the 1960s, particularly in France, another term began to prevail: the biblical term *Shoah*. The word, which first appeared in this context in 1933, means "destruction," a destruction that occurs without petition, without prayer, a destruction that occurs naturally, a destruction with no recourse to a god.

In short, as so often, each successive choice between words pitted one camp against another (Allies against Nazis, Francophones against Anglophones, Jews against goyim) until, finally, with *Shoah* and *Ḥurbān*, it pitted Jews against Jews: on the one hand, those who believe that the event is unique; on the other, those who believe that it is simply one more calamity. But, as everyone knows, two Jews, three opinions.

On this Sunday in August 1942, having spent most of the day wandering, Vicente came home just as it began to rain. He had gone home "just like that," for no apparent reason, as was the case with everything he did now. He went home, as he always did recently, without anyone knowing whether he would stay for dinner, whether he would sleep there. The girls were well-behaved. They were doing their homework. They were model students. Sometimes, sometimes even now, Vicente would look at them. And, as she saw him look, Rosita could not help but remember how much he had loved them, how much he had adored them, just as she could not help but think that he probably loved them still, even if, since receiving his mother's letter, he was unable to show them the slightest sign of affection. As for

Juan José, who was waiting for his father, constantly turning to him for attention, desperate for his father to talk to him, acknowledge him, Vicente did not even seem aware that the boy existed, that he was growing up, calling him Papá. Vicente only occasionally gave the boy a forlorn or frustrated glance, as though he particularly resented him. Though he could not formulate the thought, though he could not understand it, Vicente had gradually begun to make his son pay for the guilt he felt toward his mother, the guilt that, this year, would begin to gnaw away at his insides.

"Why don't we go out for a bite to eat?"

As Vicente never suggested anything, Rosita took the initiative. Since it was Sunday and the children had not been to school, since they had not been out all day, since it was five o'clock, since the furniture store was closed, and since Vicente happened to be at home, Rosita suggested that the five of them go to Confitería Ideal, the tearoom where her brother, Léon, introduced her to her future husband. She knew that Vicente had always loved that *salón de té* where they had first met. She knew that he admired this place decorated entirely with materials and furniture imported from Europe. Vicente knew the owner, Don Manuel, and it was he who had told them, years ago, shortly after their wedding, that the chairs in the great room had come from Prague, the chandeliers from France, the stained-glass ceiling from Italy, the oak paneling from Slovenia, and how the marble for the columns and the staircases, the beveled glass for the picture windows, the bronze for the wall sconces had all come from the great capitals of Europe—where, Vicente had made a promise to Rosita, he would one day take her.

As she walked into the great room with her husband and her children, Rosita could not help but forget the present and smile as she remembered those promises. Vicente's promises, and his constant prattle in those days. "How can he have been so effusive back then, so silver-tongued—so charming? And how can he seem to utterly forget me now?"

For his part, as he stepped into the great room with his family and looked around for a table where they could sit, Vicente was thinking of nothing. Although at home he had agreed to his wife's suggestion, although he had walked along the streets holding his daughters' hands, although for ten minutes he had been almost present, as soon as he walked through the doors of Confitería Ideal he lit a cigarette and, once again, his mind was engulfed by whiteness. He sat down and smoked, oblivious to his daughters' conversation, oblivious to his son's loneliness, oblivious to his wife's heartrending nostalgia. Once more, the outside world had ceased to exist. His thoughts were lost upon a vast snow-covered steppe. He no longer felt anything. Only the trickle of acid dripping down his throat, creating a blazing furrow that reminded him of his misfortune. Vicente felt nothing, thought nothing—except at one particular moment, when his eyes met Rosita's and she turned away to look at the tearoom: suddenly he was struck by the realization that she was remembering their first meeting, and the dozens of other times that they visited this place, about his words, about their happiness. And in that moment, he was painfully aware that all the things she remembered were true: it was true that he had once thought he would take her to Europe, just as it was true that he had loved this place, these materials—this place and these materials that reminded him of his past, and which he now despised.

Afterward, Rosita, Vicente, and the children walked home slowly. The father's silence had rubbed off on the whole family, and even five-year-old Juan José, out of unconscious imitation or respect, spent long minutes without uttering a word. At some point while they walked, the boy had reached up to take his father's hand. But Vicente had refused. The moment he felt his son's hand brush against his, almost without realizing, he pulled away and, his shoulders hunched, his head bowed, he had walked on. Seeing her son's affectionate gesture and her husband's cruel response, Rosita had had to grit her teeth to stop herself from crying. "Why? Why did he do that? Why is he never here anymore? Why does he not think of us anymore? Why does he not love us anymore? Why? Why? Why is it all over? Why does he cling to this silence that is killing us, destroying our children, our family, our love, our life?"

That evening, it took the children a long time to fall asleep. Rosita read them a bedtime story, and another, and another. Then, tired after having spent all day caring for the children by herself, she removed her makeup, brushed her teeth, and went to kiss her husband before going to bed. Vicente did not say a word, but he accepted the kiss on his forehead, and fleetingly laid his hand on hers. Rosita went off to their bedroom and Vicente sat in silence in the living room, his eyes fixed on the dark window that opened onto the little balcony, staring at the ink-black sky. He sat there for another ten minutes. Then he, too, left. He stood up, took his jacket, left the apartment, and headed out into Buenos Aires to find a poker table where he could play.

Rosita, unable to shake off the questions that had been nagging at her all day, turned off the light, but could not get to sleep: she had heard her husband leave, as he had done almost every night in the past month, and, alone in the bed, she wept for a long time, stifling her sobs with the pillow. "Why? Why does he not love me anymore? Why does he not touch me anymore? Why does he not kiss me anymore? Why does he not fuck me anymore? Why doesn't he fuck me anymore—even in silence?" Rosita continued to cry inconsolably until she heard a small voice behind her:

"Mamá?"

Martha and Ercilia were standing next to the bed, holding hands in the darkness. They were staring at her, a little upset, a little afraid.

"It's Juanjo . . . he woke up . . ."

". . . and we tried calling you, but . . ."

Rosita had not heard them. Her sobbing had drowned out their calls. She got up, apologized that she had not heard them, took her daughters in her arms, and led them back to their bedroom, where she soothed Juan José, who drifted quickly off to sleep. She again apologized to her daughters, tucked them in, and kissed them good night.

"Mamá, why are you all wet?"

Rosita had not noticed that she had cried so much her face was still wet with tears.

"What happened?"

"Nothing, nothing . . . it's nothing."

Rosita wiped her face, reassured her daughters, kissed them once again, and left the light on when she went back to bed. She left it on to comfort her daughters, and to comfort herself.

ONE EVENING IN FEBRUARY 1943, SHORTLY AFTER coming back from Mar del Plata, Vicente and Rosita were visited by a man of about thirty whom neither of them knew: Moishe Feldsher, a doctor. Dressed in a woolen jacket, a little gray scarf, and a dark hat, he rang the doorbell of their apartment one sweltering Saturday austral summer afternoon. Seeing his clothes—which were decidedly too warm for the season—Vicente knew immediately that he was only recently arrived in Buenos Aires. Moishe Feldsher was a friend of Berl's. They had worked side by side in the ghetto, which Moishe had managed to escape six months earlier. In Yiddish, he recounted the long journey that had taken him from Poland to Russia, then Finland, where he had managed to catch a ship to Brazil. After two weeks spent stuck in São Paulo, he had finally managed to get to Buenos Aires. It was Vicente's elder brother who had given him their address. Moishe Feldsher told them that Berl and his wife had been a great help when he had been deported to the Warsaw Ghetto from Berlin, and talked to them about how they had worked together:

"During the first months, we were consulted about various illnesses, mostly typhus and tuberculosis. We were working sixteen, eighteen hours a day. We tried to find ways to treat every patient, though most did not have the means to pay. Then, as supplies of medications dried up, we focused on a single disease, the only disease we were not taught about in medical school . . ."

"Oh, really—which one?" asked Rosita from the kitchen, where she was making coffee.

"Starvation."

Since Vicente was not saying a word, Rosita came back into the living room and continued to make conversation.

"But . . . I don't understand . . . Why were you never taught anything about starvation?"

"For one very simple reason: because it is the only illness that cannot be treated."

Moishe Feldsher took the cup of coffee proffered by Rosita and thanked her with a smile.

Making an immense effort to overcome the silence that

had engulfed him now for weeks and weeks, Vicente managed to articulate three words in this language he had not spoken since he left Warsaw:

"And my mother?"

Moishe Feldsher gave him news of his mother, if "news" can refer to information that is already six months out of date. At the time he managed to escape, he said, she was still alive; though very weak, she had not caught typhus or tuberculosis.

"Maybe having a son who is a doctor has its uses after all," he joked.

With a detachment that Vicente found hard to bear, Moishe Feldsher continued to talk about the ghetto, about the war, about his fiancée, who, fortunately, had managed to escape with him and was expecting their first child. Then he finished his coffee and, perhaps just as irritated by the silence of his host, he took his leave, despite the fact that Rosita had invited him to stay for dinner. Vicente barely said goodbye before turning back to the little balcony off the living room. The death throes of the day were never-ending. The sky was dark and the horizon, streaked with long pale clouds, was the color of honey and blood. The day was slowly dying. Slowly dying a bloody death.

As so often lately, Vicente had wanted to speak but had been unable. How could he possibly speak as this man had, so casually, so thoughtlessly, so affably when the fates of his mother and his brother were being played out eight thousand miles away? Shortly after Moishe Feldsher's departure, when the sky was jet black, Vicente got to his feet and, without a word, took his jacket and left the apartment. He met up with Sammy in the smoky backroom of a bar in Once where he played poker until dawn, losing every peso in his pockets. Then, instead of going home, his heart filled with shame, he had gone to the furniture store. Lying on an unsold sofa in the basement, he tried to rest for a few hours. But sleep afforded him no rest. That day, for the first time, he had a dream that he would dream again and again for the rest of his life. He dreamed he was in his own bed and, getting up, he noticed that someone had built a wall around him. He followed the line of the wall only to find himself encircled: he was walled in, completely walled in. Vicente tried to jump over, to tunnel under, to break down the wall, but it was high and unyielding. As he struggled, the wall began to creak, to move, to close in on him. It drew in until there was no space left. Vicente beat on the wall with all his strength, he shouted and struggled and suffocated and shouted again. But it was useless: the wall inched closer, suffocating him a little more. Suddenly, Vicente noticed he was holding a knife. The wall was so close now it pressed against his body, and, desperate for air, Vicente gripped the knife, to plunge it into the wall and pierce it. He managed to puncture the wall, to create a hole, a gash, and the wound began to bleed—and he felt the pain.

It was then, as he realized that the wall was his own skin, and that his only choice was to suffocate or to hack himself to death, that Vicente woke, breathless and bathed in sweat. It was almost noon. Vicente calmed himself, caught his breath, got up, and left the store. "One more Sunday," he thought as he headed home. "One futile Sunday. One more pointless Sunday to come before a Monday as futile and as pointless. One Sunday. Two Sundays. Three Sundays. A Sunday to count the Sundays. As though days and weeks still had any meaning." Vicente Rosenberg's life, like so many lives, like those of millions of Jews, of hundreds of thousands of Romani, of tens of thousands of Communists who had lost or were about to lose those nearest to them in the camps—his life, like those of all the lost souls around the world, carried on. It carried on as lives so often carry on: without a goal, utterly stripped of meaning. Vicente vaguely carried on working, vaguely carried on caring for his children, vaguely carried on loving his wife. Buenos Aires was thriving, bustling, radiant, and Vicente, in silence, carried on living without a flicker of desire, a flicker of pleasure. He would leave his apartment, walk to his furniture store, welcome customers, sell bedrooms, living rooms, dining rooms.

Sometimes he almost enjoyed it. Sometimes he almost took pleasure in this pathetic, insignificant routine. Sometimes, he almost enjoyed living, just as he—almost—enjoyed gambling until dawn and losing all the money that the store brought in. For Vicente gambled as though the sole purpose of gambling were to lose. He gambled more and more, and lost more and more. Night after night, he gambled, gambled, gambled, and he lost, lost, lost. He lost as if losing everything would be enough to pay his debts.

Rosita no longer knew what to do with her husband. "I remember when we first met. I remember his arms, his hands, his mouth. I remember that he was everything. I remember that he was he, that he was I, and I was nothing anymore. And it felt so good to be nothing anymore." Rosita allowed the wave of memory to wash over her. She thought about his hands, about his eyes, about the tongue that had tasted everything delightful in her being. The intimacy had been so intense. And so gentle. "I remember that he could never forget my body or my soul or my lips or my cheeks or what he called—what did he call it again?—oh yes, the delicate porcelain of my skin. He spoke so quickly, so beautifully, so gently, so everything. He was there. Yes, that's it. He was present. So present! He was he, and he was two, and he was ten. He was like a river or a sea or a deluge. And like a tear, too. And a stone. He was like a reef in the middle of the ocean." Rosita remembered and sometimes it made her happy, and it made her smile; and often, much more often, she remembered and this made her sad, it made her unhappy, and she cried hopelessly. "I loved him. I loved him so much. I loved him more than myself." Rosita remembered the past and she also understood, each time better than the last, what was happening in the present. She realized that Vicente could not forgive himself for not being able to save his mother, but she did not know how to help him—how to help him save his mother, obviously, or how to forgive himself. "I could try to convince him that it is not his fault, that he did everything he could . . . But what would be the point? I know that it is not true, and he knows it, too. Even if he wrote to her, years ago, to say that she had to leave Warsaw, even if he wrote to her to say he wanted her to come and live with us in Buenos Aires, he never did anything to make it happen. He knows that. He knows that he needed to do something more, that he needed to do much more than simply write to her. That he needed to go and fetch her. Or at least write to his brother and persuade him to bring her here. This is the problem: there is no point trying to allay his guilt—simply because he has every reason to feel guilty." Every day, Rosita thought about the situation in which her husband found himself, but she never thought of a solution to his problem. She believed he had been right to leave Poland, right to distance himself from his mother, from his brother, from his sister. She believed he had been right to travel far in order to grow up, to become an adult—to become himself. But she also knew that he had lied to his mother when he told her he wanted her to come live with them in Buenos Aires, just as she knew that he had lied to himself when he told himself he would save them all from the calamity he felt was looming when he left Europe. And these lies and this guilt made all conversation impossible. On the rare occasions when she had tried to broach the subject, in order to console him, to soothe him, it had only served to poison the atmosphere. And when she had tried simply to be there for him, to share his silence, it had been worse still: on the only occasion that he had accepted her silent presence next to him these past weeks, although she had said nothing, although they had sat together on the living room sofa, although she had held him for a long moment and stroked his hair, he had eventually snapped and told her she did not understand, that she could not possibly understand, that she could never understand, that to understand what was happening to him, she would have to experience what he was experiencing—but that could never happen, since her father and mother had managed to escape the pogroms, that they were still here, by her side, in Buenos Aires.

However, an incident beyond her control was about to disrupt the painful monotony of these dark days. One evening after work, a few short weeks after the visit from Dr. Moishe Feldsher, while Vicente was watching Sammy play billiards in the backroom of Café Tortoni, Ariel burst in with a broad smile on his face. It was late April 1943, and Ariel had rushed to show his friends the front page of *La Idea Sionista*: the inhabitants of the Warsaw Ghetto had taken up arms against the Germans. Ariel was elated. And Sammy and Vicente quickly joined in this euphoria. Ariel ordered champagne and they drank and they talked and they left the Tortoni and they went to the Palermo racetrack. And that evening, for the first time in months, Vicente won on the horses. He arrived home shortly before dinner with a wad of banknotes in his pocket. Rosita had looked at him, astonished, stunned by the smile that illuminated his face.

"What has happened?"

"I . . . I won . . . and . . . and there's been an uprising! The people in the ghetto have risen up! Can you believe it? They've taken up arms and killed dozens of Germans!"

Vicente's excitement not only caused him to exaggerate the number of Germans that had been killed, but allowed him to regain the use of his tongue for several minutes, to talk to his wife about what he had read in the newspaper, about what he had heard from Ariel, who had talked to his cousin, who had penned the article. His heart was filled with irrational optimism. Convinced, like many others, that the outcome of the ghetto uprising was uncertain, for the next two weeks, Vicente went back to reading newspapers and talking every day. His hope, his optimism, his jubilation, which Rosita joyfully welcomed, were at once irrational and yet rational since, for a brief moment, those living in the ghetto had genuinely mounted a resistance against the German soldiers. In fact, having learned that the mass deportations that had begun in July 1942 were bound not for labor camps in the east, but for the gas chambers of Treblinka, two Jewish organizations within the ghetto, supported by the Polish resistance, took up arms. And for a time they succeeded in halting the advance of the German army. The battle, fought street by street and house by house, would last almost a month. Meanwhile, in Buenos Aires, Vicente would once again begin to speak, and to care for his children, and to love his wife. With no news from his mother beyond what he had heard from Dr. Moishe Feldsher, he dared to hope that her fate was not sealed, that it was being decided even now on the streets of the Warsaw Ghetto.

The hope had been short-lived. On the second attempt, the German army not only retook control of the ghetto: most of the houses were razed and the insurgents decimated. On May 12, 1943, Szmul Zygielbojm, the first person to alert the world to the massacre being perpetrated by the Nazis in

Poland, committed suicide in London in protest at the lack of action by the international community. And on May 16, despite sporadic clashes that would continue into July, the police commander SS-Brigadeführer Jürgen Stroop blew up the Great Synagogue of Warsaw to celebrate the suppression of the uprising. "The synagogue was solidly built and destroying it took considerable work by the sappers and the electricians. What a marvelous sight it was! After prolonging the suspense for a moment, I shouted *Heil Hitler* and pressed the button. With a thunderous, deafening bang and a rainbow burst of colors, the fiery explosion soared toward the clouds, an unforgettable tribute to our triumph over the Jews." It was in these words—like a little boy offered a toy that goes "boom!"—that Stroop related the explosion. And that, in effect, was what it was: Stroop waited while the sappers and electricians completed their work, then pressed the detonator button that went "boom." By late spring in the northern hemisphere, most of the houses inside the ghetto, like the Great Synagogue, which had once stood without, were no more than smoldering ruins.

My darling Wincenty,

I have had no more news from you. You may have written to me but the post no longer works as it did before. Nothing works as it did before. But still I hope that this letter will reach you. Shlomo told me that he will be able to get to the other side of the wall to post it. We have sold almost everything. The furniture, the books, the clothes. But nothing has any value anymore.

What little remains, even the last ring that I kept, the one your father gave me when we first met, is worth nothing now. The only thing that has any value is food. And, like everyone else, we are hungry. It is a terrible feeling. I never believed that it was possible to be so hungry. Yesterday, Berl witnessed two men in the street beat a child for a few potatoes. The boy was no more than ten years old. They left him on the pavement, half dead.

The German soldiers come by night and burst into the apartments. They kill for no reason. They say they are doing what they have been told. Some are drunk and come armed with axes. But most wear an expression that, with the winter, has become as sorrowful as ours.

Please, Wincenty, send us whatever you can. I do not know whether it will reach us, but send it all the same. Knowing that you have sent something will feel almost as good as receiving it. I hope that Rosita and the children are well and that the store is profitable.

Your loving mother.

The first jacarandas were just beginning to dapple the blue Buenos Aires sky with their tender violet hues when Vicente received this letter from his mother. For reasons that he would never understand, the letter had taken months to arrive from Warsaw. Despite the pain, despite the worry, despite the terrible turmoil that it stirred in him, he wrote back the same day. He wrote that Rosita and the children were well, that everything was going well with the store, and, with a guilt that he had never felt before, he slipped two fifty-dollar bills into the envelope.

Having been to the post office, Vicente walked home. He had said nothing to Rosita. He did not tell her he had received another letter. How could he, how could he bring himself to repeat his mother's desperate words to his wife? That evening, Vicente did not leave the apartment to go gambling. He ate dinner with Rosita and the children without uttering a word and went to bed early. He wanted to sleep. Nothing else. He wanted to sleep and to forget. He dreamed of a sleep without words, without thoughts, without images. He dreamed of a sleep without dreams. But he drifted off and once again he dreamed the dream he had had so often since the visit from Dr. Moishe Feldsher. Waking up in bed, encircled by an impenetrable wall that closed in until it suffocated him . . . everything was the same, except that, instead of appearing in his hand as if by magic, the knife he would use to get a breath of air and to kill himself by piercing his own flesh was handed to him by his mother, who appeared as if from nowhere.

Once again, he jolted awake, panting for breath. Rosita, next to him, laid a hand on his shoulder. Still petrified, it took Vicente a moment to recognize her.

"Are you all right?"

When Vicente did not reply, Rosita made to turn on the bedside lamp. But Vicente stopped her.

"No, no, leave it . . . I'll be all right."

He took her hand and pressed it to his cheek. Rosita left the lamp off. She laid her head back on the pillow and turned to him. Still holding his wife's hand against his cheek, Vicente lay down again and turned to her. They lay, face-to-face, Rosita's hand trapped beneath his cheek, like two frightened children, their eyes open in the darkness. Vicente was thinking about his mother's letter. Remembering her words, hearing her voice, soft and lilting and a little hoarse. He could hear his mother's voice more clearly than he ever had since leaving Warsaw.

In the darkness, Rosita stared at him worriedly. Vicente seemed so distant, so helpless, so damaged. Rosita gave him a smile she hoped was reassuring—but simply looked forlorn. Moreover, Vicente scarcely responded to the smile: in fact, he barely noticed it. In that moment, his gaze transpierced the eyes of his wife as he stared into the far distance, beyond the bed, the room, the apartment, the city, beyond the ocean: in that moment, his gaze was restlessly roaming the snowbound streets of Warsaw.

Then, suddenly, shrugging off the memory of his mother and of Warsaw, Vicente found himself abruptly back in the bedroom and gazed at his wife. He stared at her as fixedly as she at him. As deeply, as desperately. And, seeing this sudden change in his expression, Rosita could not help but say:

"Talk to me."

Rosita did not know what she wanted her husband to tell her, she had no idea what he could tell her, but, gently, she asked him to talk to her. Vicente looked at her in silence for a long moment. He wanted to say something, to tell her of his suffering, of the pain his mother's letter had prompted, or at least to tell her something, to give her some inkling of what he was feeling, a few words from the letter, or even to lie, to comfort her with a white lie. He would have liked to say anything simply to let her know that he heard her, that she existed—but he could not. It was a feeling he had experienced before, when he received the previous letter from his mother, but only after he received this letter did he realize that not only did he not want to speak anymore, he could not speak anymore. He longed to speak, but, imprisoned in the ghetto of his silence, he *could* not speak. He no longer knew how.

Of this letter—the last he would receive—Vicente never said a word to his wife, to his children, or to anyone else.

ON THE DAY AFTER THIS TURBULENT NIGHT, VI-cente accompanied his wife and children to lunch with Rosita's parents, something he had done about once a month since their wedding. "La Fábrica," their house next to the workshop where the furniture was crafted, was one of the large single-story buildings typical of Buenos Aires, with a covered patio; and this monthly meal, this little family feast, was a fixture that Martha and Ercilia had already begun to look forward to, to beg for. Parents, children, grandchildren . . . often, there were at least twenty guests at table. Vicente had never really enjoyed these family meals, but he had always been happy to attend. Although (as he once jokingly told Rosita) he thought of his in-laws as "a bit hick," he was very fond of them. And now that the children were growing up, now that the girls were so excited at the prospect of seeing their countless cousins, even Vicente had begun to think of these family get-togethers as something inevitably joyous.

This Friday, as he had every time they had been to lunch in the past three years, Rosita's father, Pini Szapire—whom the cousins tautologically dubbed "Grandpa Zeide"—buttonholed Vicente before they sat down and asked him how things were going at the store. He always worried about his son-in-law, and constantly wanted to reassure himself that Vicente was working hard, and that the store he had entrusted to him was thriving. But also, he simply liked to "talk furniture."

"So, what do you think of the new credenzas we've been making from quebracho? Have you seen the finish on them?"

With an immense effort, Vicente managed to reply with brief but positive news: like every business in Buenos Aires during those years, the furniture store, though he spent less and less time there, was doing well.

Once at table, when the traditional lemon chicken with baked potatoes had been served and the children were eagerly tucking in, Vicente was returned to his suffering—and his silence. "We are hungry. It is a terrible feeling. I never believed that it was possible to be so hungry." Vicente looked at his children, at the food, and he remembered the words from his mother's last letter, the letter he had spoken of to no one. Was she still hungry? Was she hungry and thirsty right now while he and his wife and children were enjoying a delicious family meal in Buenos Aires? Why? Why did she have to endure this? Why was she not here, sitting at table with them, with the parents of his wife, with her grandchildren? Vicente looked at the chicken, at the children, at the adults, tormenting himself with these questions. And it was not just that he found no answer to them: he did not trouble to look for one. What purpose would it serve to look for an answer? The simplest questions, those whose answers seem self-evident, are often the cruelest—they are the cruelest precisely because they do not need to be asked.

Driven by thirst, I eyed a fine icicle outside the window, within hand's reach. I opened the window and broke off the icicle but at once a large, heavy guard prowling outside brutally snatched it away from me.

"*Warum?*" I asked him in my poor German.

"*Hier ist kein warum,*" he replied, pushing me inside with a shove.

Hier ist kein warum. Here there is no why. It would be many years later that Vicente would read these words by Primo Levi, these words that summed up the determination of the Nazis in the camps to create a space that was utterly different, a space in which there was no why. Every day during these dark years, Vicente, crippled by guilt in Buenos Aires, both hoped and feared he would have news of his mother, and, unable to find answers to the thousand questions tormenting his heart, he often thought that there were many things for which there was no why. Only much later, when he discovered the reality of the Shoah, did he realize that the difference was simple: in life, some things have no why; in the camps, the Nazis had stipulated, and succeeded, in ensuring that *nothing* had a why.

Before the end of the war, Vicente did not know all the things that he would learn brutally afterward. But, at the moment he read the last letter from his mother, he had been able to surmise enough that he no longer wanted to talk about it. He knew enough to decide not to keep his eyes half-closed any longer, instead, he kept them firmly closed: overnight, he once again stopped listening to the radio, reading the newspaper, paying attention to café conversations. He had decided never again to speak about this—about this, or anything else.

And in this unmoving flight, in the endless quest to know nothing, in this baleful choice of a slow lingering death, only one thing made it possible to survive: gambling. The horses, the casino—and especially the poker tables. On that Friday evening in early summer when he came home from the family lunch, as every evening, Vicente left the apartment in search of a poker table.

During the last two years of the war (and long afterward, almost until his death), gambling allowed him to survive because, sometimes, rarely, for a few hours or a few days, he could pretend that he was very rich; and, conversely, much more often, gambling allowed him to survive because it allowed him to be very poor: to lose everything and to suffer. Like his silence, his gambling would become a prison and a punishment. When he went to the racetrack, when he sat down at a poker table, or when he and Ariel and Sammy spent the weekend at the casino in Mar del Plata or Montevideo, everything seemed to fall back into place: it was no longer a question of living, of carefully building piece upon piece, it was merely a question of risking everything on the turn of a card—in the hope of losing everything on the turn of a card.

Rosita loved him enough to share his suffering, but he did not want her to share it with him. His daughters, now seven and nine, were old enough that they could begin to understand, but he did not want them to understand. Having imagined what little he could imagine as he read his mother's last letter, Vicente had resolved to say nothing and to gamble. His life, his real life, he decided, as though it deserved to be no more than a faded forgotten picture on a crumbling wall, would remain fixed in November 1943. It was in that moment that Vicente brutally became a stranger to himself. He became another, another devoid of meaning, devoid of hope, devoid of a future. But the most crucial thing, the most brutal thing that could have happened in his life did not happen. It should have happened to him, but did not. It happened to his mother, to his brother, but not to him. "I no longer want to speak. I no longer want to think. I no longer want. I no longer want anything, anything at all. I want to say nothing. Yes, to say nothing. Not a word. Not a sound. Nothing." Vicente wanted to know and did not want to know. He wanted not to know because he thought that anything he learned would be worse than his not knowing. "Listen? Why listen? Speak? Why speak? Say nothing. Know nothing. Keep it all at bay. Keep apart from the world. I have that right, don't I?"

Before that last letter, Vicente had read the newspapers. He knew that the situation in the Warsaw Ghetto was increasingly difficult, he knew that for Jews in Germany and in the occupied countries life was becoming unlivable. He had read the harrowing words in *La Nación, The Daily Telegraph, The New York Times.* Before that last letter, Vicente had read the papers searching for signs, for clues, for hints that might help him understand—and searching, like everyone else, for reasons *not to understand.* Before this last letter from his mother, like every human being, Vicente had wanted to know and, at the same time, had preferred not to know.

After this last letter, everything changed. After this last letter, Vicente wanted only to know nothing; to know nothing about anything. To be brutally, absolutely ignorant of everything. He wanted to learn what it meant not to know. He wanted to live in darkness. He wanted not to know any more, but more than that, he wanted to *no longer* know. To no longer know anything. Not even the things he already knew. He no longer wanted to know anything about what was already past and about what might happen in the future. Not to his mother, or to his brother—nor to his wife, or his children, or himself.

It is perhaps one of the most singular traits of a human being: just as the body, when it has endured too much suffering, or has grown too weak, temporarily lapses into unconsciousness so that, like a machine, it can restart, fire up again, so the mind, when pain and hopelessness become too much, grows dark, grows deaf, closes in on itself so it can survive, or rather so that something can survive—something that is at once still human and already less than human, something that is still ourselves and is already no one.

After this last letter, Vicente stopped believing. He stopped believing in everything. In his wife, in his children, in himself. He stopped believing that life was more important than death.

And yet, after this last letter, just as after the flicker of hope sparked by the Warsaw Ghetto uprising, life, once again, resumed its course. It resumed its infinitely slow, infinitely futile course. Vicente no longer felt like doing anything. Yet every morning he got up. Every day he went to work. Every day he lived his family life, immured in silence, and every night he gambled. He gambled in order to punish himself—and in order to forget. Even if he could not manage to forget. Ariel would often tell him that he had to forget, that he had no choice, that he had to think about something else, that he had to shake off this melancholy that was killing him, that he had to do it for his wife, for his children. That he had to focus on his work. That he had to forget and also, and especially, that he had to stop gambling—that he had to stop losing everything.

Vicente listened to the advice of the friend he had known since adolescence, but he gave no answer. He knew that he had to forget. He knew that he had to stop gambling. He knew that he had to make an effort for Rosita, for Ercilia, for Martha, for Juan José, but he was incapable of making even the slightest effort. The only thing that he still hoped, on the rare occasions that he still hoped, was that one morning he would wake up after a night of gambling that left him so exhausted and so penniless that, when he woke, he would have forgotten everything. Would have forgotten everything, unwittingly, unintentionally, inadvertently. He dreamed of waking one morning and remembering only that he had once known something he no longer knew: remembering, as so often happens in life, that he had forgotten something, but without knowing what it was he had forgotten.

But this morning never came. Vicente dreamed of a new dawn, but every dawn he woke to was the same: the same memories, the same guilt, the same longing to forget.

But then, one day, although Vicente had not spoken in months, although he no longer went to the Tortoni, although he no longer did anything but work in the store in silence (or rather pretend to work as he watched Yorgos, his assistant, actually work), Ariel and Sammy came to the store to show him various newspapers filled with photographs of celebrations in the streets of Paris—which had just been liberated. Vicente did not really react, he did not say anything to his friends, he showed no particular sign of happiness or regret. But, going home that evening, he was a little more affectionate toward Rosita, and that night, after they had put the children to bed, they did something that they had not done in many months: they made love. It was early September 1944.

The following morning, at once fearful and firm, Rosita told him that she had decided to take up her pharmacy studies again.

"I know you are against the idea. I know that you don't want me to. But I can't carry on, Vicente. I'm suffocating. I'm suffocating in this apartment. I need to get out. I need to do something else. I've asked my father and he will lend me the money so we can pay for a nanny to help out with the children."

Rosita looked at her husband, waiting for a word, a reaction, a refusal. At the very least, she thought, he would be furious that she had borrowed money from her father. But once again, Vicente said nothing.

"The fact that you want to die, that you want to let yourself die as though the world had ceased to exist, as though nothing matters anymore, not even the children, that is your business. But I refuse to accept it. I refuse to die with you."

Again, Rosita stared at him. Again, she waited. But Vicente simply bowed his head and heaved a long sigh. And that morning, as the late winter sun caressed the streets of Buenos Aires, it was Rosita who left the apartment to go for a walk.

Vicente could have tried to respond, but he did not try to respond. He could have tried to stop her, but he did not try to stop her. He could have tried to understand what his wife had said on this morning, after a night when love had triumphed briefly over silence and death, but he did not try to understand. He did not try to respond, to stop her, or to understand because, in his eyes, after that night of love, nothing mattered anymore. The little flicker of joy he had felt when he learned of the liberation of Paris, like the vast hope he had felt during the few weeks the Warsaw Ghetto uprising lasted, was due partly to the fact that he still hoped his mother was alive. He hoped for a reason that was at once irrational and yet rational: because no one had yet told him that she was dead.

"If you don't mind, I'll sleep at the store . . ."

"Again?"

The austral winter was coming to an end and spring was beginning to animate the city streets with shouts and laughter, but Vicente felt more and more alone. At night, before leaving the apartment to go gambling, he would sometimes tell Rosita that he would not be home.

"I'm having trouble sleeping at the moment."

On the pretext that he needed quiet, and preferred the cool dark store after playing poker, he slept in the basement stockroom more and more often. And more and more often he had the dream he had first dreamed after the visit from Dr. Moishe Feldsher. Now, in the dream, he would examine the wall that had been built around him. When the wall began to close in, he would study the stones, touch them, feel the humidity seeping through the chinks. He no longer raged against the wall, no longer pounded on it with his hands, his fists. He contemplated it, inspected it, surveyed it as though the death it portended no longer really concerned him. But there always came a moment when, the wall having closed to the point that he had no air, he would find himself with a knife, a hammer, sometimes even a sledgehammer—and at that point he would brutally demolish it.

And he would always wake in the instant that he realized that this wall encircling him, suffocating him, this wall he furiously stabbed at and destroyed was his own flesh.

The liberation of Paris had been followed by the liberation of Belgium and the Netherlands, by the Allied advance into Germany, and the Red Army's capture of Warsaw. But, once again, Vicente showed no interest in what was happening in Europe. He had returned to his prison of silence—and gambling.

On a particularly dark Saturday in late October 1944, Vicente headed on his own to a particularly seedy bar down by the docks. He had spent the whole night gambling and losing. He had lost. And lost. And lost again. And when he had lost everything, on this particularly dark night, in this particularly seedy bar, he had managed to persuade a particularly disreputable player to lend him a little money—which he also lost. At dawn, he had been allowed to leave only because the owner of the bar knew him, and knew Ariel and Sammy, who, he also knew, would pay his debts if necessary.

Vicente walked back along the docks to the city. As he crossed the railway tracks, he encountered a raucous group of young people leaving a party in a building in El Bajo. They were disheveled and excited. There were only ten of them, but they bellowed and roared like a crowd of thirty. As they emerged from the building, they jostled Vicente without realizing. They were too excited. So engrossed were the boys by the girls, the girls by the boys, that no one in the group stopped to apologize. No one even seemed to notice this lone, pale, haggard man wandering lost in the soft glow of dawn. As they wandered away through the arcades, drunk, garrulous, stumbling, and smoking, Vicente recognized one of the boys walking arm in arm with a girl: it was Franz, his young German assistant. Vicente stared after him for a long moment. He looked so happy, so carefree. Franz had not noticed him. He simply disappeared around the corner with his friends.

Vicente stood for a moment, confused and unable even to begin to understand his confusion. Then he had carried on his way. He had coffee at the bar of Café Tortoni and left as it began to rain. Avenida de Mayo was leaden and gray: the shuttered stores, the motorcars, the rare pedestrians, everything seemed gray, heavy, and sad, as though about to crumble. "Duty. Duty. It's a duty. A necessary obligation. A necessary obligation to dutifully do something. To do something to counter the nothing that I do." Vicente walked on, head bowed, staring at his feet as they moved one in front of the other to a rhythm as regular as it was vain. He walked slowly along the sidewalk as the avenue became unending. Exhausted, beaten, he walked on, and walked on, and all around him the buildings crumbled and dissolved in the rain like walls of sand. "Something must be done to counter the nothing that I can do. I can do nothing. I cannot do anything. I have never understood the difference." Like tadpoles, words without tails once more began to wriggle in his mind. And he tried desperately to follow a thread that fatally eluded him. "Or live again. Stop losing. Live again, yes. Be a man again. A real man. The captain. A man who lives. A man who speaks. A friend, a husband, a father. A . . . a child. To be. Once more. A child." At these words, these thoughts so loud he believed he could hear them, Vicente felt tears begin to trickle down his cheeks. "The bustle of the world. The bustle of the world or the streets the cafés the park the trees the wind the children the school. Life that was life. But life has disappeared. It has slowly slipped away. And I don't know where it is now. I am alone. I no longer hear. My ears are closed like my eyelids. The sun is rising and I am sinking. I am sinking, I know, I am sinking. And I am falling. I fall like the night, like the world. From where, I do not know, but I fall. Slowly I fall. Gravely I fall toward my grave. Yes. That's it. That's enough." As he walked, Vicente's feet had unconsciously led him to the store. It was seven fifteen, it was Sunday, and he had absolutely no reason to be here. Yet, mechanically, Vicente rolled up the metal shutter. Yet, mechanically, he let himself into the store. Not yet knowing what he wanted, what he was searching for, Vicente went down into the basement, into the stockroom where he often slept. But this time, he did not look at the unsold sofa that had so often served as a bed. Vicente looked for a rope he remembered having seen in one of the large crates that had been delivered a few days earlier. He found it, and made a slipknot. He threaded the rope over one of the thick metal pipes that ran along the ceiling, took one of the New Style chairs from a job lot of fifty he had never managed to sell. "Arms folded, mouth closed. I cannot carry on. But it's simple. End it. Leave. Disappear once and for all. Die. Die slowly but die at last. Die a peaceful death. An easy death. My death. Die my own easy peaceful death." Vicente stood on the chair and slipped the rope around his neck. "Yes. Yes. Let my death be peaceful—even if I die."

Vicente closed his eyes and stood for a moment on the chair without thinking. He stood for a moment in silence.

Utter silence. Not a single word formed in his mind. He was calm, relaxed. He was not even thinking that he had finally stopped tormenting himself. He was not even thinking that he had finally stopped thinking. Death, before he died, had already allayed the anxiety that, for months, had prevented him from living. Vicente felt no doubts, he felt not the slightest hesitation: he knew he was going to die. He was there. Finally there.

Faced with his own death, he was finally himself—and already he was no one.

A step. Two steps . . . Three.

Vicente had already braced himself to kick away the chair when he heard the hesitant footsteps of someone entering the store. Curious, quite simply curious, he managed to stop himself. He pricked up his ears and listened; it was not so much that he wanted to know who it could be, he simply did not want to make a noise. He was disturbed by the absurd notion that someone might hear the chair clatter on the floor, come down to the basement, and see his corpse. It disturbed him as though it were possible for him to feel shame even after death. And so he stood motionless on the chair, listening intently, and he waited. There was little doubt that this person wandering through the dawn in Buenos Aires, this intruder who had no reason to be here, would quickly leave. He waited patiently, standing on the chair. He waited in silence, careful not to make the slightest sound.

"Vicente?"

Vicente could not help but start as he recognized Rosita's voice. "What the . . . Why? How can . . . ? What is she doing here? It's not possible. It's simply not possible that . . ." Abruptly, words once again began to form in his brain. Language had returned, like a raging torrent—at once exhilarating and terrorizing.

Vicente could not see his wife: he could simply hear her footsteps slowly approaching the trapdoor that led down to the cellar.

"Darling?"

Vicente did not answer. But he suddenly began to sob. His brain was once again overwhelmed by a jumble of thoughts. The rope still around his neck, tears and snot began to stream down his face. And his heart, filled with shame, no longer knew what fate awaited.

Bringing his hands up to his face, he tried to muffle his sobs, but Rosita had already heard. She stopped on the lip of the trapdoor. From the moment she found the front door open, she had known Vicente was in the store. Now she stood waiting at the top of the ladder that led down to the stockroom. Vicente could clearly see her shadow fall across the steps.

"Vicente . . . ? I . . . I wanted to say . . . that I . . . I just wanted to tell you that I'm pregnant, darling."

ARLY 1945, AS THE END OF THE WAR LOOMED, THE newspapers, even in Argentina, increasingly began to talk about the fate of the Jews in Europe. In order not to know what he could have known at the time, when the last Germans were driven from Poland, when the Soviets were liberating Auschwitz, Vicente kept his eyes tightly shut. Wanting not to know, wanting to *no longer* know, wanting to no longer know anything, even the things he already knew, he locked himself away in a silence that was increasingly onerous, increasingly dense, a silence buried deep within his belly that had now grown like a cancerous tumor, gradually metastasizing to his chest, his lungs, his throat, his brain.

The effort it required to not know had become his sole reason for living. So, when he finally knew, Vicente was devastated. Because everything he suspected—everything he could and *could not* imagine in 1943 and 1944—was less terrible than the truth.

Before 1945, Vicente had not wanted to imagine what the camps people had begun to talk about were like. He had not wanted to wonder whether they looked like a prison, a mental hospital, or a cattle market. He had not wanted to imagine whether prisoners wore uniforms or whether they were naked. He had refused to imagine his mother being beaten with rifle butts, dragged by the hair through the frozen mud, or tortured to make her confess to things she did not know. Vicente had refused to ascribe images to this reality, this reality that no one, it seemed, had truly witnessed—one that those who claimed to have seen it could not understand, one that those who claimed to understand could not explain.

Vicente had not wanted to know. He had not wanted to imagine. But in 1945, like everyone else—gradually and in spite of himself—he began to know, and could not stop himself imagining. Gradually, he wondered what his mother felt imprisoned behind the ghetto walls. Wondered what she had thought of the overcrowded streets, the beggars, the sickly children. Wondered how she had endured the cold, the hunger. Wondered how she could survive not knowing—or worse, *knowing*—what would become of her. Howling with rage and despair, he wondered how she got through the deportation, being transported in a cattle truck, how she had walked down the corridor, how she had reacted when ordered to undress, how she had undressed.

Gradually, as he struggled not to know, struggled not to imagine, Vicente was forced to live a very different horror from the *ultimately brief* horrors of Treblinka: the horror of a life of guilt, a life in which guilt daily ate away at him, the horror of having escaped, having abandoned his mother, having fallen short in his destiny, the horror of not being where he should have been—even if it were only to die alongside her.

Did she cry when they dragged her out of the house? Did she scream? How did she react when she was loaded onto the train? What was she imagining when they told her to undress? What did she say? How did she feel? What did she think? Did she still have the strength to speak, to feel, to think? Vicente did everything in his power not to know, not to imagine, but gradually he came to know and the jumble of terrifying images became imprinted on his mind. Cold, tremulous images that would gradually freeze into a single image, one image from which he could not escape, an image that would forever be imprinted on his eyelids when he closed his eyes, and when he opened them again: the image of his mother's naked body, as he had never seen her, as he would never have wanted to see her, an image of her wretched body, worn by age and fear, lost amid a multitude of other wretched bodies, of her body, arms outstretched as if to protect herself, her body and those emaciated legs, swept along by dozens, hundreds, thousands of other legs just as emaciated—an image of his mother, naked, among countless feeble, skeletal bodies, beaten by rifle butts, urged on toward the showers. If there was a single image that Vicente wished he had never imagined, one that, from the moment he first read the descriptions of the camps, he would never forget, it was the image of his mother, naked, drained, exhausted, as she stepped into those showers that were not showers.

All through Rosita's pregnancy, Vicente could not help but learn more and more about what had happened in Europe. But still he said nothing. He would never tell anyone about his mother's last letter. Nor about her death. He would never tell Rosita, never tell his children—even later, when they had grown up—when and how his mother had died, when and how his brother had died. Vicente would never choose to share his suffering in order to assuage it, never want his family to live in the futile cruelty of memory.

Vicente had been settled: forty years old, married, with two daughters and a son, with friends, a thriving furniture store, and a city that no longer felt alien. He had been a man like so many others, happy and unhappy, lucky and unlucky, energetic, tired, present, absent, sometimes care-free, sometimes passionate, rarely indifferent. He had been a man like so many others but now, suddenly, though nothing about his circumstances had changed, nothing about his daily routine had changed, everything changed. He was a fugitive, a traitor. A coward. He had become the man who was not where he should have been, the man who had fled, who had lived while all around his people died. And from that moment, Vicente chose to live like a ghost, silent and alone.

In the summer of 1945, at the invitation of Rosita's parents, Vicente had agreed to vacation with his children in Mar del Plata. He had tried to join in his children's joy as they played on the beach. Tried to stay away from the casino. Tried to be grateful to his in-laws. And he had tried, though he did not say a word, to show affection for his wife, who was four months pregnant.

Then he and the family returned to Buenos Aires. And, once again, life resumed its course. Vicente went back to working; the children went back to school. Rosita did not go back to university as she had planned. In March 1944, when Juan José started elementary school, her home life had been so complicated, and Vicente so clearly unable to care for the children, that she had decided to defer until the following year. But the following year, Rosita fell pregnant. And her dream of going back to university was filed away in a drawer, never to reemerge.

Shortly after the school term began, on March 27, 1945—preposterous as this may sound—Argentina declared war on Germany. Vicente was no longer the young dandy he had been. He was an enfeebled man, terribly enfeebled. He had lost almost all of his hair, and his bald pate constantly seemed to weigh on him. His eyes, once green, had changed color, and were now an aqueous gray. In the space of four years, this elegant, graceful young man had become an aging family man. Sammy and Ariel said nothing to Vicente. But when they talked among themselves, they often wondered how Vicente had managed to age so much in only four years. This did not stop them from loving their friend as they had always done. The three would still meet at Café Tortoni at the end of the day, still make occasional trips to the racetrack, where luck could turn. But Sammy and Ariel avoided going with Vicente to play poker—where, whatever happened, he always succeeded in losing everything he had won earlier.

On the evening of May 8, 1945, as it rained over Buenos Aires and the children were already in bed, the radio play that Rosita was listening to in the kitchen was interrupted by a newsflash that the armistice had just been signed. Ercilia was ten, Martha eight, Juan José seven. And Rosita was eight months pregnant. Vicente had not spoken to a living soul in weeks and weeks. Not to Sammy or Ariel, not to his wife, nor to his children.

In the living room where he was sitting on the sofa pretending to read a book, Vicente could not help but overhear the news. He listened for a moment, until the news bulletin ended and the play resumed, then set down his book and got to his feet. He went into the kitchen, walked over to his wife, and gently laid a hand on her belly.

"*Mi Rusita . . .*"

Astonished at these words, the first words her husband had uttered in months, Rosita gazed at Vicente for a long moment in silence.

"Yes, my love?"

"If it's a girl, we will call her Victoria."

Rosita laid her hand on her husband's and, tears in her eyes, she nodded.

Victoria was born on June 17, 1945.

1945.

Seventeen years later, Ercilia fell pregnant and I, in turn, was born. Martha became my aunt, Juanjo my uncle—Vicente and Rosita became my grandparents.

Victoria became the youngest of my aunts, the one to whom, six years later, after she had moved to London, I would write my first letter.

I do not know precisely when Vicente found out that his mother had been deported to Treblinka II, a camp where there was never any question of labor, where no one died of fatigue, exhaustion, or starvation; this camp that had been the most efficient of them all, this camp that had been an implacable machine designed to kill as many people as possible as swiftly as possible—this camp where, in the space of a year, the Nazis had managed to exterminate almost a million people. But I know that he knew. Just as he knew that the Nazis took Berl's five-year-old son and deported him to Auschwitz. Just as he knew that, despite their hardships, his brother and sister-in-law had carried on working until the Warsaw Ghetto uprising, in which they participated, and which cost them their lives.

"It was such a pleasure to receive your letter with the photograph of Rosita and the baby. I am so happy to see your happiness, the love you share, and your beautiful little girl." "It has been a long time since I last wrote to you. I have been ill, so ill that I lost my memory and could not write." "I wanted to ask whether it would be possible for you to send a parcel of warm clothes, woolen sweaters, pants, gloves, and wide, low-heeled shoes, size 5. There is no news here. We are in good health. Life is painful. Death is everywhere."

I have read many, many letters written by my great-grandmother Gustawa Goldwag, though, of course, I never knew her. In 1997, on the one and only occasion I visited the tourist ruins of Auschwitz, I wrote a poem to her. A poem that is not very good.

Nor can I truly say that I knew Vicente and Rosita well: my grandfather died in August 1969, when I was seven years old; my grandmother in March 1980, when I was eighteen.

I do not know whether, before he died, Vicente realized

that remaining silent was not a solution. I do not know what he thought about the Shoah, this event which from having no name came to have too many. I do not know whether he thought that the choice of the name *Shoah* was a way of stating that there never was and never could be an equivalent, that it is unique, incomparable, unparalleled in scope—that it is unimaginable. I do not know whether, worn down by his own silence, he came to think, as I do now, that if we are not to be complicit in the Nazis' attempted murder of language, we must at all costs think this unthinkable.

Adorno said that to write poetry after the Holocaust was *barbaric*—only to reconsider and return to writing. Does the Shoah have a *definitive quality*? I find it difficult to say that anything has a "definitive" quality. Like Pythagoras, like Borges, I prefer to think that things cyclically return. Anti-Semitism forced my forebears to flee Europe. Latin American dictatorships forced me to flee Argentina and later Uruguay with my parents—to return to Europe. I was forced to leave my country, my mother tongue, my friends. Like my grandfather, I was a traitor: I was not where I should have been. But I am not complaining. This has been my life. The only one that I have lived. And I like the fact that my flight was also a return. I discovered things my grandparents had known, and others they had never known. I learned that the world is wide, that languages are multiple. I forgot a little Spanish, I learned French. And while I never truly liked living in France, I cannot lie: I like writing in French.

Martha's eldest son, Martín Caparrós—always known in the family as Mopi—when recounting the life of our grandfather Vicente Rosenberg, a few years before me, wrote:

> The Shoah is part of our shared history: in a way that is unendurable, it defines what it means to be human. For years, I had known this story only from afar: I had watched films and seen photographs, read studies and accounts. I was horrified. I asked myself questions to which there were no answers. Then I realized that my great-grandmother died there and that this story was also my story: the story of my blood.

Do we truly carry, in this liquid that can keep us alive or can kill us, stories that can be put into words? I have often claimed in my writings that I was writing only in order to survive my past. I have often written that forgetting is more important than remembering. Like Pasolini, I have often thought that those who forget are happier than those who remember. Yet today, as night falls over Paris, as the setting sun streaks the sky with the same blood and honey with which it stained the skies of Buenos Aires seventy years ago, and, exhausted from another day spent providing light for a species that is forever human, forever barbaric, as it darts its dying rays through the windows of my study, I who have never liked neither memory nor blood, long to say that Mopi is right. I want to believe that the same blood flows through his veins and mine; through the veins of my brother, and my cousins, Gonzalo and Miguel, who are like brothers to me, and my cousins Lila, Manuela, and Natasha, whom I love like sisters and also grew up with. And through the veins of Ariel, the son of Juanjo, with whom I have lost touch. As I grow older, I want to believe that something of my past lives on in me—just as something of me will, I hope, live on in my children.

I want to believe that Vicente and Rosita live on in me, that they will continue to live on after I am gone—that they will live on in the memory of my children who never knew them, and in these words that, thanks to my elder cousin, I have been able to address to them.

A NOTE FROM THE TRANSLATOR

There are some novels where the greatest challenge is not translating the words but the silences between them. Santiago H. Amigorena's *The Ghetto Within*, like his earlier autofictions, is pervaded by stillness and silence, even as the world is wracked by war and fear. Recreating the cadence and rhythm of his prose in English involved not simply listening intently to what was said but to what was left unsaid.

As I worked on this translation, I was also attentive to the tremors and vibrations of the other languages that roil and seethe beneath the French, since *The Ghetto Within* has as its genesis two enforced exiles separated by half a century. Anti-Semitism forced his grandfather Vicente to flee Poland for Argentina and later consumed his country and much of his family; in turn, the brutal dictatorships of South America forced Santiago's parents to flee for post-war Europe for France. It felt appropriate and in keeping with Amigorena's polyglot heritage to include flashes of porteño Spanish to his descriptions of a city where I, too, was fortunate to live for a time, and to restore the Polish orthography of some names and places, like glittering shards of memory.

Most of all, I have tried to capture the voice of his grandfather; his words and his grieved silences, his fears and his qualms as a young man reinventing himself, striving to fashion a new life even as the old is being razed.

—Frank Wynne

Here ends Santiago H. Amigorena's
The Ghetto Within.

The first edition of this book was
printed and bound at LSC Communications
in Harrisonburg, Virginia, August 2022

A NOTE ON THE TYPE

The text of this novel was set in Adobe Garamond
Pro, a typeface designed in 1989 by Robert Slimbach.
It was based on two distinctive examples of the
French Renaissance style: a Roman type by Claude
Garamond (1499–1561) and an Italic type by Robert
Granjon (1513–1590). The typeface was developed after
Slimbach studied the fifteenth-century equipment at
the Plantin-Moretus Museum in Antwerp, Belgium.
Adobe Garamond Pro faithfully captures the original
Garamond's grace and clarity, and it is used exten-
sively in print for its elegance and readability.

HarperVia

An imprint dedicated to publishing international voices,
offering readers a chance to encounter other lives and other
points of view via the language of the imagination.